The Secret of
Sambatyon

To Zvi Berkowitz
Hope these adventure
sweep you off to a
wild reading

The Secret of Sambatyon

The Adventures of
EMES Junior Interpol

By

Gershon Winkler

Illustrated by
Lloyd Bloom

The Judaica Press
New York
1987

Library of Congress Catalog Card Nos.
87-080550 Hardbound Edition
87-80195 Softbound Edition

ISBN:
0-910818-68-1 Hardbound Edition
0-910818-69-X Softbound Edition

For additional information, write:
THE JUDAICA PRESS, INC.
521 Fifth Avenue
New York, N.Y. 10017

Manufactured in the United States of America

Table of Contents

Author's Acknowledgement

I am very grateful to Jack Goldman, President of Judaica Press, Inc., for the opportunity to write yet another book for the Judaica Youth Series.

Believe it or not, writing a book for youth is far more complicated and challenging for me than writing one for adults. And so I owe a debt of gratitude to my dear friend and mentor Devorah Podrabinek, who inspired the idea of weaving the Midrashic legends of Sambatyon into the adventures of Emes Junior Interpol.

Finally, I thank Bonnie Goldman for doing a superb editing job on this book and for courageously coaxing me to make it a better, more meaty adventure story.

Thanks to you all.

Gershon Winkler

About The Author

Gershon Winkler is the author of *The Golem of Prague, Dybbuk, Soul of the Matter* and *The Hostage Torah*.

He is currently involved in teaching, writing and research.

CHAPTER 1

The Wounded Pelican
in the Galilee

Simcha was elated. He had dis-
covered the solution to all of the world's problems. All of them,
mind you! And the feeling was one of total, absolute fulfillment,
complete satisfaction. After all, now that all of the world's problems were solved, there was nothing ahead but undisturbed
peace and tranquility. Farewell problems! Good-bye suffering!
Have a nice trip, *tsores*[1]. You see, all that needed to be done was
to turn over all of the stones in the entire world. It would be a
cinch. Volunteers from across the globe could be gathered within
a few weeks and the stones could be turned over in maybe a
few months. As each stone was turned over the world would
start to improve right then and there. What a revelation! Simcha
couldn't wait to wake up and tell Moshe.

"Turn over all the stones, eh?" Moshe later teased him.
"What a dream! If it only were true!"

"Maybe it is true," mumbled Simcha as he washed his face
in the rushing creek. The two had been camping in the Galil,
the heavily wooded mountains of northern Israel; a place where

[1]*tsores*—problems [Yiddish].

7

prophets once walked and where dreams could be as enchanting as the scenery. "I mean, it felt so real, at least while I was dreaming. Just turn over all the stones in the world, and all of the world's problems are instantly solved. Poof!"

"Poof is right," chuckled Moshe as he folded his sleeping bag. "You're taking your dreams too seriously."

"Hey, don't knock it. I mean, the Talmud teaches that one-sixtieth of a dream is prophecy. Maybe it was prophecy," insisted Simcha.

"Or maybe it was a *baba meise*[2]. Remember you once told me the silly things the kids in your yeshiva[3] class used to say?" said Moshe, ever the Israeli skeptic.

Simcha stood with his hands on his waist, an annoyed look on his tanned face. "What silly things?"

"You know, like if you could manage to kiss your elbow, the *Moshiach*[4] would come," said Moshe with a sarcastic laugh.

"Oh, those silly things." Simcha smiled. He hated when Moshe teased him. But there was no point in becoming angry. They were just different. Simcha was intrigued with mysticism, and Moshe preferred hard, cold facts.

"Yup. And it doesn't sound any less reasonable than your dream about the stones."

"But maybe, just maybe… I mean, kissing your elbow is impossible. But turning over a stone isn't that difficult."

"Yeah, but turning over every stone in the entire world is like trying to kiss your elbow."

There was a pause for what seemed to be a long time. They stood amidst their camping gear gazing at one another. The two boys had met by chance a few years ago on an airplane travelling from New York to Israel. Simcha was going to spend the remainder of his high school years in an Israeli yeshiva. Moshe, an

---

[2]*baba meise*—old wives' tale or unbelievable story [Yiddish].
[3]*yeshiva*—religious school for the study of the Bible, Talmud and Jewish law.
[4]*Moshiach*—messiah [Hebrew].

Israeli, was returning from a year in New York where he had been an exchange student in a New York public high school. They became fast friends—and partners. They discovered that together they had a unique talent for solving mysteries. They called their detective team Emes[5] Junior Interpol, and they soon had a growing reputation among family and friends. But they came from different backgrounds. Simcha was the son of an Orthodox rabbi, and he himself was quite religious. Moshe, on the other hand, was raised secularly and, before he had met Simcha, had been anti-religious. Their meeting and ensuing friendship had changed this, and Moshe soon joined Simcha in the Jerusalem yeshiva. But sometimes it was difficult for Moshe to understand Simcha's sometimes mystical mind.

"I can't believe you've got me taking this dream of yours so seriously," laughed Moshe. "I mean, for the past fifteen minutes we've been discussing nothing but stones and improving the world. How did I get involved in this?"

"I was wondering how long it would take for you to realize I was fooling around with you," laughed Simcha. "You take me too seriously sometimes."

"I don't know when you're joking and when you're not! Anyway, does the Talmud really say that about dreams, I mean, about their being one-sixtieth prophecy?"

"Yes. That's what it says. Why?"

"Well," Moshe began, a sly, mischievous smile breaking on his lips, "I had a dream last night that I poured a canteen of water over your head!" Moshe suddenly grabbed his canteen and dashed toward Simcha. Simcha quickly took flight, running up some rocks and deeper into the woods, laughing hysterically, with Moshe in hot pursuit. Simcha zigzagged around some trees and ran back down the hill, where he spotted a cave. Quickly turning his head, Simcha realized Moshe was rapidly catching

[5]*Emes*—which in Hebrew means truth, was formed from the first letter of each of their first names [MS].

up, so he slipped into the dark cave where he came to a halt and surrendered to Moshe's water assault. "Hey! Not so much!" screamed Simcha as Moshe thrust the open canteen of water in his direction. "Remember, only one-sixtieth! That means only a drop! Just a drop! Hey!"

Suddenly the boys stood still. A strange noise that sounded like a scream seemed to be coming from the back of the dark cave. The two remained standing in the pitch black for what seemed an eternity.

"Let's get out of here," whispered Moshe.

"Shhh. I wonder what it was," said Simcha. "What a strange sound."

"I say, let's get out of here! Can't we discuss how strange the sound was when we get home?"

"Shhh. Listen. There's something struggling in there."

"I'm getting out of here, Simcha. Coming?" said Moshe uneasily.

"Shhh! I'm really curious. Wonder what it is." Simcha had closed his eyes and was trying hard to listen.

"It's probably just some stone that turned itself over. Your curiosity could get us in big trouble. Now let's go!"

"I just heard something again. Give me your flashlight."

Moshe unhooked his flashlight from his canteen belt and handed it to Simcha. Simcha switched on the light and then suddenly stepped back, almost knocking Moshe down. There, in the light, they saw the source of the strange sounds—a wounded pelican limping frantically, trying to evade the two intruders. "A pelican!" said Moshe, moving a few steps closer for a better look. "What's a pelican doing in a cave in the Galil? They're usually found by the ocean. That's at least twenty miles from here."

"It's strange, all right," said Simcha, remaining still. "I wouldn't advise you to step any closer to it, though. It's obviously wounded or something. It's not a good idea to go near a

wounded animal. They're liable to attack you."

"Hah!" said Moshe, retreating to where Simcha stood. "Are people that much different? Ever go near somebody who's in a bad mood? Grrrrr. They'll attack you without warning."

The bird limped in a nest of dry leaves, every now and then lifting its left wing and weakly waving it about.

"I bet it was flying south for the winter and then hurt its wing," said Simcha. "Look how it's flapping the left one about."

"What are we going to do? Ever fixed a wing before?" said Moshe, smirking.

"Nope. I guess there really isn't anything we can do for it. I mean, if we tried to take it to a veterinarian, we'd probably need medical help ourselves by the time we got there."

"You're not kidding. Look at the size of that beak, eh?"

"Look, at least we can leave some food and water for it, you know? Maybe it just needs a rest and the wing will heal itself. Got some bread left, Moshe?"

"Sure. I even have a whole tuna sandwich left. These guys love fish."

The boys left the cave and walked through the woods back to where they had camped. While Simcha completed the chore of packing up the gear, Moshe wrapped up several slices of bread, including his tuna sandwich, and returned to the cave. Simcha was just about finished buckling his backpack when he heard Moshe's call pierce the steady sound of the trickling creek. Simcha jumped to his feet and hurried through the woods toward the cave. As he ran, he prepared himself for the worst. Had the bird attacked his friend? Had Moshe fallen into some pit along the way? Did he sprain his ankle? Had Simcha's innocent curiosity endangered his best friend? The faster he ran the more terrifying were his thoughts. Arriving at the mouth of the cave he was relieved to find Moshe standing there in one piece, still grasping the food and water he had prepared for the bird.

"What happened?" shouted Simcha, still fearing something amiss.

"It's gone! The bird is gone! Poof! Disappeared! Just like that!" exclaimed Moshe. "I got here just five minutes ago, walked into the cave real slowly so as not to frighten it, and it wasn't here. I looked outside and nothing. I mean, how far could it have gone?"

Simcha entered the cave and walked cautiously to where the bird had been nestled earlier. Holding the flashlight, Moshe followed a few steps behind him. As Simcha drew closer to the spot where the bird had been, he noticed something glittering in reflected light partially hidden by dry leaves. He pushed the leaves aside and picked up a small, antiquated coin-like object with the faded engraving of a tree on it. "Look!" he exclaimed excitedly, momentarily forgetting about the bird. "Look what I found, Moshe. It looks like some kind of ancient coin."

The boys walked out of the cave to examine the coin in the light of the sun. "What do you think it is?" asked Moshe. "Think it's from a long time ago?"

"Looks weird for a coin, I'd say. Didn't they have engravings of the face of the king or emperor way back? But a tree?"

Simcha turned the coin over and scraped away a layer of clay which had adhered to its surface, exposing some tiny ancient Hebraic symbols. "Wow. This looks like Hebrew, but it's different. Look at the lettering. It looks so familiar, and yet I can't make it out. Can you?" Moshe took the coin and squinted, trying to decipher the strange symbols. "Looks like Hebrew characters alright," he said. "But I can't make it out either. Unless it's just some initials, or something like that. Wait. This here is an *alef*, right? Look at it." Simcha grimaced as he strained his eyes and then nodded. "Uh huh. Could be, could be."

"Hey, I got it. I think, but I'm not sure, that the next letter is a *shin*. Right? What do you think? It's hard to tell, you know. It's so faded. Think that could be a *shin*?"

Simcha's head was beginning to hurt from squinting and straining. "Whatever you say, Moshe. It's giving me a headache, so you better do all the guessing."

"Now the next letter is a tough one. See how it seems to be scratched? It could be a *vav*, or maybe a *resh*, or maybe a..."

"Just a second, Moshe. Let me see that coin again," exclaimed Simcha suddenly. He took the coin and turned it from one side to another like some kind of expert. "It is probably a *resh*."

"Why do you say that?"

"*Alef, shin, resh*, would spell *asher*."

"So?"

"So Asher was the name of one of the twelve sons of Jacob, one of the twelve tribes of Israel. Their symbol, if I remember correctly, was a tree. Put two and two together and you get a coin or some kind of token from the tribe or region of Asher."

"Wow. It must really be old, then. Maybe more than two thousand years old!"

"And we would never have found it were it not for that bird," said Simcha.

"Oh, yeah. I almost forgot all about the bird. Wonder where it went," Moshe said.

"Hmmm. Maybe it wasn't real," mused Simcha. "Maybe it was there just to draw our attention to this ancient coin."

"*Baba meise* time again! What's so important about an ancient coin?" Moshe was becoming irritated with Simcha's tendency to find meaning and mystery in everything.

"I don't know. But that bird looked too sick to fly away. This is too weird to have no meaning at all, don't you think? I mean, we're awake, you know. This is no dream."

"If we could only find that bird," said Moshe. "The entire mystery would be resolved."

"Sure. We'd ask the bird to tell us all about the coin, right? How would that solve anything?"

"It would at least shatter your theory that the bird wasn't

really a bird. Do you think that it was some kind of angel trying to bring the coin to your attention?" Moshe said, rolling his blue eyes. "I think you've been out in the woods too long, Simcha. Let's forget this whole thing and head back. My father's expecting us back in Jerusalem tonight, remember? We've got some walking to do before we even see a bicycle, let alone a bus. We can take the coin to some museum person. You know, a curator, or whatever they call them. Maybe it's worth a fortune. If it is, I promise I'll believe all your theories."

The boys walked back to their campsite and then, after helping each other secure their packs on their backs, they began the hike back to the trail. Clouds were forming above them, darkening the mountains, almost making it seem like twilight. The two walked briskly over fallen branches and huge stones, heading toward an open field which would take them back to their path. As they passed several rocks, Moshe couldn't resist his impulse to ask Simcha why he wasn't turning them over one by one as he passed them. Simcha smiled and was thinking of a good retort to his friend's chiding when lightning lit up the dark grey sky and a sudden roaring clap of thunder shook the hills, sending shocking vibrations up through their spines. Before they could react to the deafening noise, torrents of rain needled down upon them, drenching their clothes and gear within seconds. The boys ran for cover in the clefts of the rocky canyon which bordered the open field. A second clap of thunder, louder and more fierce than the first, blasted the summit of the nearby mountains, followed by a powerful gust of wind which howled through the trees, sending leaves and branches flying past the narrow refuge the boys had found for themselves.

"We gotta get home by tonight, Simcha. I promised my father."

"I know, but it's dangerous to move around in this weather. I'm sure your father will understand if we get to Jerusalem a few hours later."

"This is very strange weather, don't you think? I mean, there were no clouds out earlier, and then suddenly this storm drops in on us."

"Maybe we'll be lucky and it'll disappear as quickly as that mysterious pelican."

"Gee, I hope that bird is all right. Hope it isn't caught in the storm or something."

The boys huddled in the small refuge of the rocky canyon, each lost in his own thoughts.

"You really think that coin is from Asher?" asked Moshe.

"I think so. We'll know for sure when we show it to an expert," answered Simcha.

"Whatever happened to those guys anyway? You don't hear much about the tribe of Asher. Or any of the other tribes for that matter. All you hear about is Judah, Levi, maybe Benjamin. Sometimes Joseph, I guess. Actually, not even Joseph's tribe. Or Naftali. Or any of the others."

"Well," said Simcha, dodging a flying twig, "they got lost. They were driven out of Israel around the time of the destruction of the first Holy Temple. And they haven't been heard from since. That's why they call them 'the ten lost tribes.'"

"We found one of the lost tribes, though," said Moshe, wiping his wet nose with his wet sleeve. "You know, the Black Jews living in Ethiopia."

"That's right. Isn't that something? It apears they are from the tribe of Dan."

"I wonder if we'll ever discover the rest of them?"

"With time I'm sure we will. The Ethiopian Jews were discovered about three hundred years ago, you know. There is reference to them in the writings of several rabbis back then."

"You think the other tribes are living as isolated and distant from one another as the Ethiopian Jews were?"

"Gee, I don't know," Simcha said thoughtfully. "But there is a *midrash*[6] about the ten lost tribes living together somewhere

[6]*midrash*—a collection of interpretations of the Bible by Rabbis, compiled through many centuries, from about 2,000 years ago to about 800 years ago.

in the deepest, darkest part of Africa. They are supposedly living near a legendary river the *midrash* calls 'Sambatyon.' According to this legend they are led by the daughter of... of..." Simcha's eyes widened and his face lit up. "You won't believe this, Moshe..."

"The daughter of who?"

"The daughter of Asher!" Simcha exclaimed watching a look of surprise cross Moshe's face.

"You're kidding!"

"Nope. The daughter of Asher, no less. Her name is Serach."

"But how can she still be alive?"

"Well, according to this *midrash*, Jacob blessed her with everlasting life. When Joseph's brothers came back from Egypt with the news that Joseph was still alive, Serach was the first to tell Jacob about it. Jacob, in disbelief, jokingly told her that if Joseph was alive, she'd live forever. And so it happened according to the *midrash*. I guess the words of a spiritual giant like Jacob stick!"

"That's fascinating. Do you think it's really true? You know, what the *midrash* says about all that? I mean, it sounds so fantastic. Like science fiction."

"Could be real and literal, could be allegorical. I guess we won't know for a while. But that's not the end of it!"

"There's more to this?"

"Uh huh."

"Well, before you go on, Simcha, let me ask you this—if there really is such a place where the lost tribes are living, what stops us from going there? Why haven't the Jews tried to discover this Sambatyon place?"

"That's what I was about to explain, Moshe. See, according to the same *midrash*, large boulders rain down on this river Sambatyon, making it impossible to travel there. It also says that the rocks only cease their assault on Shabbos[7].

[7]*Shabbos*—Friday sunset to Saturday sunset. Work and normal daily activity are stopped during this time among religious Jews.

"Sounds too cute to me, Simcha, with all due respect to the *midrash*. I think it's some kind of allegory. It's too wild. A woman thousands of years old, an ancient tribe of Jews living in the deepest, darkest, most dangerous rock-sliding regions of Africa. Come on, Simcha. Do you really believe this stuff about Sambatyon?"

"I've never really given it much thought. My father used to tell me about it when I was little," Simcha said shrugging. "Maybe you're right. Maybe it has some deeper meaning and is not to be taken literally. Who knows? Maybe it's symbolic, just like this coin is symbolic of something. This coin of the tribe of Asher."

"Well, Simcha, hang on to that coin. You never know. You might bump into Serach one day, and she may be able to use it to make a phone call!"

The two boys laughed. The storm seemed to have subsided. Only a light drizzle fell now, and the clouds were moving on. They rose and resumed their journey.

CHAPTER 2
Of Plans and Keys

Colonel Tamari paced nervously back and forth in his office, the telephone pressed tightly against his ear.

"Well, what am I supposed to do?" he shouted into the phone. "I can't just march into an Ethiopian refugee camp and walk out with seven hundred Ethiopian Jews trailing behind me!... What?... Bribes, *shmibes*... I said bribes, *shmibes!* Even if we bribed the officials with a billion shekels each, word would get out in no time at all, and we'd be stopped at the border or on the road. It's impossible, I'm telling you... I know, I know, I'm not saying that you haven't tried diplomatic channels. I'm only telling you that I appreciate your confidence that I can march into Ethiopia with a couple of agents and walk out with seven hundred Ethiopian Jews and a brass band... I'm telling you I can't! It's just not that easy. Why can't the army handle it? It would be another Entebbe to them!... What do you mean I'm not in my right mind!... I'm a what?... Listen, Shmueli, I've got a few good names for you too... What?... No, I'm not turning my back on anyone! It's just not that simple! It'll take weeks of planning... What? I can't hear you so well... What? Can't you speak a little louder? What's wrong with you? Speak up!... No, I'm not going to turn off my air-conditioner! You just have to speak louder!... I'm a what?..."

Just then, Ella, Tamari's secretary, entered and placed an envelope on his desk. The colonel waved his free hand at her in a gesture of thanks and picked up the envelope. Noticing the sender's address, he sat down behind his desk, the telephone now positioned between his shoulder and jawbone, and opened the letter. "Uh huh, uh huh..." he mumbled into the phone, though his attention was now focused on the contents of the letter. "Sure, sure... Yeah, that's right, you're absolutely right... I know exactly what you mean... Uh huh... Sure, Shmueli. Sure... Sure... Uh huh... Yeah, okay, I'll get back to you with a plan real soon... sure. Okay, good-bye. Shalom, my friend... What did you call me?... A what?... Listen, you know...... Hello? Hello?... Aaaa, good-bye!"

He slammed the phone down so hard that it cracked. His eyes still fixed on the letter in front of him, Colonel Tamari reread it from the beginning, a smile of triumph slowly spreading across his face. He called his secretary through the intercom. "Ella, get me a flight to Nairobi. Uh... make it for me and my wife! Uh, make it for next Monday. Tourist class. And make twelve separate reservations for the men of Squadron-Zayin. Yes, each a different hotel, and, you know, put some in business, some in tourist class: you figure out something. Yes, that's it. Have them travel different days but I need them all in Nairobi by next Thursday the latest. That's it. Thanks..."

The door to Tamari's office buzzed open, and in walked Simcha and Moshe. Tamari took one quick look at the two and dialed Ella once more. "Make that *four* tickets for my party... Yeah, four: me, my wife, and the last two people I would ever leave behind in Israel without a hundred guards watching their every move... That's right, Ella, Simcha Goldman and Moshe

you-know-who, that infamous self-employed detective team...
Who knows? Don't worry. I'll think of something to keep them
busy there... What?... Oh, don't be so concerned, Ella. I'd be
worried more if I left them here alone. These two think they can
just run around solving mysteries, worrying their parents half
to death! You remember the trouble they got into in Egypt? And
don't forget the mess they fell into chasing that elusive pirate,
what's-his-name, in Georgia[1]... What kind of mischief could
they possibly get into in Africa?... What?... I can't hear you
well, Ella, please speak a little louder... What?... I don't want
to turn off my air-conditioner! Just speak louder!... Safari? You
mean the one in Ramat Gan? No? Hahahaha! What a splendid
idea. Send our heroes on a long African safari. It's brilliant, Ella!
Not only will they be out of my hair, but they'd be so far removed
from any trouble-making opportunities that it would even be
safer than having them locked up in a vault. You're brilliant,
Ella. You're a real life saver. Thanks!"

The colonel hung up and smiled broadly at the boys who
had been standing near his desk listening with great interest.
Moshe was running his hand up and down the conspicuous
crack on the telephone while Simcha was furiously scratching
his arm at a left-over mosquito bite he had brought with him
from the Galilee camping trip.

"You're not really going to do that to us, are you, *Abba*[2]?"
asked Moshe, now taking a closer look at the damaged telephone. "If you have to go to Africa, I'll be okay. Simcha and I
will find things to do."

"That's precisely why you're going on a safari," Tamari
exclaimed as he stirred his coffee. "I'm afraid that you two *will*
find something to do. By the way, when does the yeshiva start
up again?"

---

[1]Details of their exciting adventures can be found in *The Hostage Torah, The
Egyptian Star*, and *The Floating Minyan*, all published by the Judaica Press.
[2]*Abba*—Father [Hebrew].

"In about three weeks," said Simcha. "But really, Colonel, there's no need for you to spend extra government funds to take us along."

"Are you serious? The government would be more than willing to spend *twice* as much. Can you imagine how nervous the country has been over the last two days while you two were alone in the Galil? No, seriously, I've got some money put away for just such a trip."

"Ah come on, *Abba*," laughed Moshe, still examining the strange crack on the telephone. "We didn't get into any trouble in the mountains. I mean, what could possibly have happened on a camping trip?"

"You are right, my son, absolutely right. You two proved beyond the shadow of a doubt that nothing could possibly happen, no mischief, no insane adventures, while you're out on an innocent camping trip. That's why you two are going on yet another camping trip, a long camping trip, into the innocent jungles of Africa. On a nice, quiet, relaxing, trouble-free safari."

The boys eyed each other and shrugged. What could be so terrible, they realized almost simultaneously, about going off on a safari in Africa? Neither had ever been further on the African continent than Egypt, and the idea began to seem attractive, the more they thought about it. Tamari studied the boys' reaction and waited for them to say something. He couldn't understand why they weren't excited. Why they weren't jumping up and down, screaming and clapping each other on the back. Why they were just standing there in silence?

"Fine," said Moshe. Simcha nodded in agreement. "We'll go to Africa with you and take the safari," he said. "Sounds pretty interesting, I guess."

"Sounds pretty interesting, you guess?" Tamari repeated, puzzled. "I'd have thought two guys like you would have been shouting with joy about such an opportunity. Have you two been through so much danger and adventure already that nothing excites you anymore?"

"No, *Abba*, it's not that," explained Moshe. "It's just that we just came back from two days of hiking in the mountains. So we're kind of tired. A safari, as great as it sounds, seems like a pretty tiring adventure, if you think about it from our point of view."

"I can understand you boys are tired and need some time to nurse your blistered feet back into shape. Did you think I was going to fly you to Africa first thing tomorrow morning and send you off on a safari the moment you stepped off the plane? Certainly not. You'll have a few days of rest here before flying to Nairobi, and then I'll get rid of... uh,... I mean then I'll arrange the safari."

"*Abba*, what happened to the telephone?" asked Moshe, still caressing the gaping crack.

"Oh that? Nothing really. They just... uh... they just don't make telephones the way they used to. That's all. Okay, boys, that's enough for now, unless there was any specific reason you came to the office today."

"How come you have to go to Africa, *Abba?*" Moshe inquired suddenly.

"Oh, nothing special. Just a little vacation from all this work piled on my desk." The colonel shook his head in dismay as he glanced down at his desk. "Look at all these papers. Just look at them. In fact, I'm taking your step-mother along, see? So it's an... uh... you know, a vacation. Nothing more. Now answer my question. Why did you come up here today? Something on your minds?"

"If you're going on a vacation, does that mean you're coming along for the safari, too?" Moshe asked.

The colonel rose from his desk and walked to the water cooler with an empty paper cup. He filled the cup with water and gulped it down while trying to think of something to say. Tamari, usually tight-lipped and unruffled by anyone's questions, often found his son the most difficult to answer. "Uh... well, I promised Esther we'd do some touring together, just she and I. You understand, Moshe. You know that since we were married a few months ago, I haven't been able to spend much time alone with her. Does that answer your question? Now, tell me, what's on your scheming little minds?" Tamari asked, eyeing the boys brightly.

Moshe smiled slyly and then boldly replied, "*Abba*, I know you're also going to Africa to help the Ethiopian Jews come to Israel. I just want to tell you how proud I am that you're finally going to help them!"

Tamari almost choked on his water. He gazed wonderingly at his son and sat down slowly at his desk. "How in the world?" he exclaimed. "Who told you I was going to Africa to do anything of the sort?"

"It's none of my business, *Abba*," said Moshe, "but out of curiosity, why did you tell the person on the phone that you couldn't be of any help right now, and then tell Ella to make all those reservations?"

Tamari sputtered water, some all over the desk. He stood upright again and banged his fist on the table. Moshe suddenly realized how the telephone had gotten cracked. His father was having a difficult day. He eyed the desk to see whether a crack had formed. There was none.

"I guess they still make desks like they used to, eh, *Abba?*" commented Moshe a little timidly.

The colonel shot back a sharp disapproving look and then sat down and took a deep breath as he leaned back in his chair. "Okay, you guys, let me hear it. Were you deliberately eavesdropping?"

"No, Colonel," Simcha volunteered. "You were talking so loud we couldn't help but hear. No one else was in the waiting room and Ella didn't have her air conditioner switched on."

Colonel Tamari looked at the boys in exasperation. Then he

nervously ran his hand through his thick hair. "It's a good thing we don't have a loudspeaker outside the building so that all of Jerusalem could hear my phone conversations!" Tamari said as he reached for a cigarette. He lit it and inhaled deeply. "Anyway, I'll explain it all some other time. Now what did you two come here for?"

"But, *Abba*, how are you going to smuggle the Jews out of Ethiopia?" Moshe couldn't stop himself from blurting out. He knew his father would be angry, but he was really curious.

"It's no use," Tamari sighed, throwing his arms up. "I'll never find out why you boys came here unless I explain everything! Okay, what can I lose? You two will be miles away on a safari anyway." He paused, shaking his head at his son's bright blue expectant eyes. "The story is, Shmueli, the *nudnik*[3] I was on the phone with, is a straight government man. He goes strictly by the rules. I do, too, of course, but perhaps I just know a different book of rules.

"Now, there are these crazy young Americans in California who have been planning a way to smuggle the African Jews out of Ethiopia to Israel. The Ethiopian government, as you know, is not fond of the Jews there, nor is it fond of Israel. The Ethiopian Jews, in fact, are even called by the derogatory term, Falashas.[4] Anyway, Israel strongly objects to independent groups like these Americans doing what they're planning to do. We feel their interference can spoil what we have been trying to do there for quite some time now. But we believe that they are going to try carrying out their mission whether we like it or not... so why not put our heads and energies together and work as a team? Right? So I just received a telegram from the Californian group, a couple of Jewish hippies, or whatever they call them. We have a plan and we're going for it." Tamari paused, wearily smiling at his son. "Does that satisfy you? Remember, Shmueli must

[3]*nudnik*—a nuisance, a pest [Yiddish].
[4]*Falashas*—outcasts

never know about my cooperating with these American daredevils. That's the story." Tamari took another puff of his cigarette and then stubbed it out.

"What's the plan?" asked Moshe.

"Oh no, you don't," Tamari shot back. "That's all you're getting out of me, you scoundrels. Now it's your turn to tell me why you're here. I'm desperately curious."

The boys looked at each other and giggled.

"We just came for the keys to the house, *Abba*," Moshe explained. "We're locked out and *Imma*[5] isn't home."

The colonel's mouth fell open, and in exasperation, he let out a loud groan.

[5]*Imma*—Mother [Hebrew].

CHAPTER 3

Traitor

Moshe peered out from the rounded airplane window at the black, star-speckled sky and wondered why there were not as many stars as there were Jews in the world. After all, he remembered learning that G-d had promised there would be as many Jews in the world as there are stars in the heavens. He turned to Simcha, who sat beside him, reading.

"Simcha, I'm sorry to disturb you, but I have a good question for you."

Simcha shut the book on his index finger and turned to his companion. The two were seated directly behind Colonel Asher Tamari and his new wife Esther, both of whom were engrossed in their magazines.

"Your question," Simcha replied, "better be more interesting than the stuff I'm reading in this book."

"Well, I bet my question is one you've probably asked long ago back in America at your yeshiva. The Torah says that the

27

Jewish people will be as numerous as the stars in the heavens, right? Well, look out there and tell me whether you see more stars than Jews."

"I think the question should be the other way around, Moshe. Why so many stars and so few Jews in the world?"

"So many stars? What? Where?"

"First of all, pal, you're only looking at a small fraction of the galaxy, remember? There are more stars out there than meet your eyes. Secondly, our galaxy itself is only a tiny fragment of the entire universe, with its endless arrays of galaxies and star clusters each with their own massive number of stars."

"Okay, have it your way. Then why aren't there as many Jews in the world as there are billions of stars, like G-d promised? On the contrary, we are a minority."

"Good question. But I think the wording of that promise in the Torah means that the number of Jews in the world will be *as* the number of stars: just as the number of stars cannot be accounted for, so the number of Jews in the world cannot be accounted for. We cannot count all the stars in the universe because not all of them can be seen. And, in the same way, we can't count all the Jews in the world, because we don't know where all of them are. There are many Jews, for example, who don't even know they're Jewish. There are also Jews in remote regions of the world of whom we are not even aware. Remember about the ten lost tribes? For some hundreds of years we didn't know about the Jews in Ethiopia, remember?"

"Yeah, like the rabbi was telling us before the summer—you know—about the lost sparks of Israel being gathered together slowly here and there and..."

The boys were suddenly interrupted by Colonel Tamari, who had turned around in his seat and was looking at the two with an annoyed expression on his face. "Don't you two ever stop talking philosophy? Get some sleep already. I don't want to have to carry your weary bodies on my shoulders when we arrive in

Nairobi. You're probably keeping everyone on the plane wide awake with all your talking."

"Hey!" an irritated voice shouted from the rear of the plane. "Keep your voice down, mister, will you? We're trying to sleep!"

"See what you boys did?" Tamari declared: "You made me wake that guy up."

The boys chuckled to themselves and reclined silently in their seats. Simcha's mind now took him back to the United States, to his home in New York City. He tried to picture the expression on his mother's face as she read his letter about the trip to Africa.

"So what's this?" he imagined his mother saying to his father. "My son in Africa? On a safari? What kind of *meshugas*[1] is that? Going to Egypt to chase after smugglers wasn't enough for him? Almost drowning in the Atlantic Ocean while looking for a Jewish pirate in Georgia was also not exciting enough? Now he goes off to the jungles of Africa? My son the monkey, swinging from trees by his *tzitzis*.[2] Did you ever?"

Simcha now pictured his father seated in the dining room, poring over a stack of talmudic books. "Don't get so excited, Mama," he imagined his father saying, "he'll probably be staying in a big city that looks like New York or Tel Aviv. So don't worry so much. As for the safari, probably they have some safe, closed-off park for tourists, like Adventureland, you know what I mean? I'm certain he won't be going on one of those real safaris. So don't worry so much. It was very nice for Colonel Tamari to offer to take him in the first place, and I think it will be an interesting experience for Simcha."

"Don't worry so much, he tells me, don't worry so much! I'm his mother and I shouldn't worry? My son goes off to Africa and I shouldn't worry? What about the wild animals?"

"I'm sure the big cities of Africa are not fitting habitats for

---

[1]*meshugas*—stupidity [Yiddish].

[2]*tzitzis*—four-cornered fringed garment that is worn by Orthodox Jewish men who are more than thirteen years old [Hebrew].

anything wilder than an alleycat and a couple of stray dogs, just like here. So don't worry."

Simcha smiled at the imaginary scenario and then dozed off smiling, some 35,000 feet above the ground. When he awoke hours later he was still smiling, which was quite embarrassing. Opening his eyes slowly, he became aware of people moving busily in the aisles, removing their baggage from the overhead compartments and making their way toward the exits. He quickly rose and sleepily followed Moshe out of the plane.

Tamari had reserved a rented car, which was parked in front of the terminal building. Still dazed, Simcha was astonished by the wide variety of space-age gadgets which adorned the interior of the late-model sedan, and was relieved by the cool air which blew out of the car's air-conditioning system and drove the Nairobi heat off his face. Nairobi, he realized, was significantly further south than Israel and, therefore, significantly hotter.

Arriving at a luxurious hotel building, the boys were assigned their own room down the hall from the colonel and his wife. The room was freshly scented and extraordinarily neat. The voices of Hebrew-speaking men in the hallway could be heard throughout the next morning, for, as Moshe had once explained to Simcha, Israeli intelligence had officers stationed in certain parts of Africa year-round. These officers were now meeting with Moshe's father to discuss their current mission.

Simcha was flabbergasted by the scene outside his window, which overlooked the vast city of Nairobi and its cluttered but somewhat modern streets. As in Egypt, the streets were blanketed with merchants shouting about their wares as well as beggars in pursuit of food and shade. Fancy European automobiles made their way through the winding, crowded streets, missing pedestrians by what seemed from the hotel window to be a hairbreadth. The boys couldn't wait to step outside and tour the city.

As the boys stood gazing out the window, Yossi, Colonel

Tamari's aide, walked into the room to see if they had all they needed. He then carefully lifted the phone off the receiver and thoroughly inspected it to make sure it wasn't being tapped.

"Standard procedure," he reassured them. "We check the phones when on a journey anywhere, any time... You boys are expected in the colonel's suite within ten minutes. Got it?"

"Got it," snapped Moshe. "Ten minutes flat, on the button."

In ten minutes the boys were in Tamari's suite, which by this time resembled a conference hall more than a hotel room. Esther was seated on the sofa beside another Israeli woman, the wife of one of Tamari's Nairobi contacts who lived as a businessman there. The two became fast friends and found that they had a great deal in common. Their animated conversation about local shopping bargains pleased the colonel immensely, for he now felt secure that his wife would be in good, comfortable company while he was in Ethiopia.

Tamari turned to the boys to discuss their safari, placing a cigarette between his lips and lighting a match. When he noticed his new wife throwing admonishing glances at him, he immediately blew out the match, removed the cigarette from his mouth and looked sheepishly at his assistant who stood wearing a puzzled expression. "She won't let me smoke," Tamari mumbled defeatedly. "New wife, new rules, you know how it is, Lieutenant."

Tamari turned quickly to the boys, changing the subject. "As for you two, you're scheduled to go on your safari first thing on Sunday morning. You are going with three guides. They'll take you a little way into the jungle and game parks, show you some trees, a couple of animals, a bird here and there, maybe an ant or two, right? I'm just asking you to cooperate with your guides. They're being paid well to take you on this safari. Please try to enjoy yourselves. I have enough to worry about now, and I don't want to have to interrupt my mission here to fish you two out of some trouble. Okay?"

"Trouble?" the boys exclaimed. "Us?" They looked at one another with mocking expressions of innocence and then looked at the colonel, who was waiting for their response.

"Okay, *Ha'mefaked*[3]!" the two replied aloud in military fashion. Tamari smiled. If only his own men would respond so obediently and with such snappiness, he mused. But of course, this was not the Israeli army, and even in *Tzahal*[4], the outward trappings of military discipline were only superficially obeyed. Yossi ushered the boys back to their room. In the hallway Moshe remarked about his father not trusting them. "What do you mean?" asked Simcha. "Your father was just joking around about all that trouble-seeking jive."

"It's not that. I meant the fact that my father has to send us on a safari with three guides. *Three* Kenyans? We don't need an entire company to take us! What's wrong with one, or even two? But *three*. Sounds like we're going to be watched pretty carefully, or like we're being assigned babysitters or something!"

"Look, your father knows what's best, Moshe. Maybe it's safer that way. Maybe if a lion or some hyenas are walking around, they'll be less likely to attack if they see a larger group of people!"

Moshe shrugged. "Yeah, I guess you're right. Maybe I'm making more out of this than it really is."

Yossi left them at the entrance to their room and returned to Tamari's suite. As he passed the elevator lobby, a short Kenyan in military garb carrying a black attaché case stopped at Tamari's door. Yossi questioned him briefly and then let him in. Tamari rose when the short black man entered and returned his salute. "At ease, Samoa," he said almost immediately, aware that, unlike Israeli soldiers, the soldiers of other countries are extremely fearful of high-ranking officers. Samoa relaxed and pulled a large envelope from his briefcase. He handed it to Tamari.

[3]*ha'mefaked*—commander (Hebrew).
[4]*Tzahal*—Israeli Army [Hebrew].

"These are your papers, Colonel," he said. "They will give you authorization to enter and leave any region in this part of Africa except, of course, Ethiopia itself. But you will have our full cooperation in this part of the continent. The papers also authorize you to carry arms. If you are ever searched or questioned—and the same goes for any of your men—you need only display these papers, Sir."

Tamari took the envelope from Samoa and studied its contents carefully. Then, a smile spreading across his face, he quipped: "They forgot to include authorization to acquire free liquor."

Samoa smiled. Then, jumping to attention, he asked Tamari if there was anything else he needed. "No, Samoa, you're dismissed," he replied. "Thanks for everything." Samoa saluted and held his hand to his forehead until Tamari returned the salute. Making a sharp about-face, the African soldier left the room.

Once in his jeep, Samoa sighed with relief. He hated these errands. Most of all, he despised having to salute the enemy. Because, in fact, Samoa sympathized with the Palestinian terrorists who waged sporadic, often deadly battles against Israel, planting bombs in Israeli marketplaces, on buses, along roads, and elsewhere. The guerrillas also waged a different kind of war within Israel, a propaganda war, bombarding Arab villages in Israel with leaflets containing false accusations against the Jewish people and the Israeli government. Although Samoa had no personal stake in whether the Palestinians achieved their goals or not, he had been promised a leadership position in Uganda, where the Palestinian guerrillas did some of their training, in return for his help.

But the task of playing the dual role of a loyal Nairobi military officer and terrorist spy was becoming increasingly taxing on the little man, and often he would go for a day or two without eating. Who, after all, could have any kind of appetite while bouncing between friend and foe, having to constantly force smiles which were not meant, and to exhibit gestures of friendliness and respect to those who were considered the enemy? Facing Tamari was one of the most difficult tasks for Samoa, more stressful than facing Nairobi government officials. After all, Tamari was an Israeli officer of high rank, and eleven months of intensive anti-Israel indoctrination by the guerrillas, plus heaps of dollars, had effectively transformed him into a full-blown anti-Semite.

Speeding around the curving streets of Nairobi, Samoa nervously eyed his rear-view mirror. He was always anxious about the possibility of being followed, of being found out. How long could this facade last anyhow? Sooner or later Nairobi intelligence would discover his real identity and aims. Eventually, they would discover that he had been supplying Tamari with travel information that would lead him and the rescued Ethiopian Jews into an ambush that none of them could ever survive. It wouldn't be long thereafter, he feared, before Nairobi intelligence realized Tamari had been set up and he, Samoa, would be their prime suspect. And if Nairobi didn't figure it out, Israeli intelligence certainly would.

Samoa took out his handkerchief and wiped the perspiration from his brow. He perspired not so much on account of the blazing heat as from the haunting thoughts of being caught. With each such trip to the enemy he felt as though he was taking his life into his own hands. Each trip was full of fear of the unknown, fear of being caught. He could hardly look them in the eyes anymore for fear they would spot the guilt in his own. Moreover, as a junior officer in his country's army, it was no simple task juggling his schedule and appearances. He had to search for cracks and crevices of time to sneak away from his duties as a Kenyan soldier to carry out his obligations to the Palestinian unit in the jungle. Sometimes he felt schizophrenic. Other times he nearly forgot whose side he was on.

"I can't do this anymore," he protested before Major Saud at the Palestinian guerrilla unit later that evening. He wiped the sweat from his forehead as he watched the concerned look on his superior's face. It wasn't even hot any longer, but for Samoa it was hell. He was becoming a nervous wreck. "Can't you select someone else for a while?"

Major Saud nodded his head in what seemed to Samoa to be sympathy, but then suddenly struck Samoa across the face, sending Samoa to the ground within inches of the campfire. Samoa didn't dare rise. He remained on the ground, his arms held over his face in defense. The major closed in on him, his face twisted in anger, his eyes small, brown and threatening.

"You back out now, Samoa," the major warned, his voice tense and low, "and I'll have you tied to a tree in lion country overnight. Hear me? You are the only one in this operation who has any official contact with the government militia, and, therefore, with Tamari. You know how important this mission is to us. Tamari is head of Israeli intelligence, and we've been trying for years to get rid of him without risking Israeli revenge. This is the ideal opportunity. Must I repeat myself to you again and again? He is here on a mission to rescue Ethiopian Jews and smuggle them to Israel. And as everyone knows, refugees from Ethiopia have often been attacked along the road by bandits. If we can ambush Tamari during his mission, no one will consider blaming us. There will be no ferocious revenge against us. They will simply assume it was the work of the highway bandits so plentiful along the route he must take. I know you're nervous, but you must learn to keep your nerves under control. You must continue to supervise the routes Tamari takes in his mission so we can execute the ambush. Understand?"

Samoa nodded and rose slowly to his feet, brushing the leaves and sand from his uniform. The major continued to stare angrily at him a few moments more before turning around and walking toward his tent. Samoa picked up his beret and walked defeatedly back to his jeep, still shaking from the incident. The slap on the face had infuriated Samoa to the point where he actually felt the impulse to defect to the Zionists and confess. But he knew better than to do a stupid thing like that. First, Saud would get him eventually. Secondly, he believed the Palestinian guerrilla cause was an important one, and if he saw his mission to completion, the rewards would be worth it all. He would not only achieve a prestigious position within the unit, but he would also earn the chance to become a government official of some sort in Uganda once the African guerrillas recaptured it. Anyway, if he confessed to the Nairobi officials he would surely be imprisoned for life—if he was lucky. They certainly would not allow him to remain an officer, and the best he could hope for would be a jail sentence, rather than a firing squad.

Samoa drove off into the jungle again, along the path leading back to Nairobi. He was expected at Tamari's suite at four in the morning for the final mission briefing. Samoa, after all, had been assigned by the Kenyan high command to be Tamari's guide into and out of Ethiopia. Samoa swallowed hard and bit his lower lip. It was going to be a long couple of weeks. Very, very long.

CHAPTER 4
On Safari

Simcha felt drowsy as the land-rover bumped up and down along the dirt road that cut through the jungle. The sun was beating down strongly upon the vehicle, its rays causing the boys and the three guides to sweat profusely. The deeper they drove into the jungle, it seemed, the more damp and hot the air became. The boys had never been in a jungle before, and they had insisted that before beginning their safari, the guides take them for a four-day hike at the game parks where most of the animals were located. Colonel Tamari had agreed to their plan.

The truck came to an abrupt halt and the guides motioned to the boys to step out and gather their gear. This was it. The end of the road. From here on, they were told, it was jungle, jungle and more jungle. No more jeep rides, no more conveniences, no more civilization.

"Oh boy," complained Simcha as he lazily slung his sleeping-bag over his shoulder. "Here we go again."

"Yup," Moshe agreed. "Another hike. We sure will be well-prepared for Israeli basic training after all this. First we go camping in the Galil, and now we're trekking through the jungles of Africa."

"I don't know, Moshe, but this much I can tell you: I'd rather be hiking around on a mission of rescue, like your father's on right now, than be on this safari."

Waikiki, the head guide, a tall, muscular Kenyan with a wide, warm smile, helped the boys fasten their hiking gear, making sure it wasn't too tightly strapped, thus preventing heat-chafing and blisters. They then set off into the thick jungle. Waikiki and the other two guides, Jono and Nick, were slashing at the tall brush with their machetes. Simcha's eyes searched the lush greenery for wildlife, anticipating the sudden leap of a panther or the frightening sight of a boa constrictor sliding up to the group for lunch. The Kenyans, noticing the anxiety of the boys as they moved stealthily on, smiled, knowing that most wild animals were to be found deeper in the forest, miles from the main road, and that not many were active during the day anyhow. But seeing how the boys were lost in their fanciful, self-created mood of suspense, they decided not to tell them anything.

The hours went by rather quickly as the boys became almost hypnotized by the endless number of leafy tropical trees and the rhythmic sounds from the birds and other wildlife that lived among them. Various small birds of flashing colors screamed in song, screeching warning signals to birds in other trees, as the group made its way past their trees. In the distance they heard the shrilling yelps of baboons at play and the yammering voices of countless other species, sounding off as if they were all part of a large, somewhat disorganized orchestra. At times they would also hear terrifying sounds from the brush, some of which resembled cries from wildcats or wolves. The boys stayed as close as they could to the three Kenyan guides as they grew increasingly frightened. As they got deeper into the jungle, it seemed to grow darker as the spaces between trees became fewer and fewer. The thick wavy branches and leaves blotted out the light of the sun, and an eerie feeling crept through the noisy wilderness.

Simcha and Moshe felt they were now at the mercy of the powers of nature, for here was a part of man's world where he was hardly welcome, and constantly in jeopardy. The boys now no longer concerned themselves with the humid heat, nor did they feel the soreness of their leg muscles or the cutting of their knapsack straps against their soft shoulders. They concentrated only on their prospect for survival, on the frightening possibilities suggested by the as yet unknown creatures issuing the terrifying sounds they were hearing. It was paradise, but it was a forbidden paradise. Or so it seemed.

The Kenyan guides, Simcha noticed, were not in the least anxious, accustomed as they were to the sounds of the jungle. To them, the howling of strange, unseen tree creatures was as familiar as was the chirping of sparrows to people living in Brooklyn or Haifa. But at the same time, the deeper they ventured into the brush the more the guides grew tense.

"Look!" Simcha shouted in a terrified voice, pointing toward a thick vine. "A snake!"

The guides motioned to the boys that they should just continue walking. The snake, Waikiki explained in sometimes awkward, but mostly good English, was totally harmless. "It's only a grass snake," he said. "A poisonous snake can be distinguished by the pit between its eyes. Usually. There are exceptions, you know. There are also snakes which may not be poisonous, but they are huge and kill their prey by strangling them and swallowing them alive. Relax, boys. No need to be alarmed unless we are."

Simcha and Moshe laughed nervously and the group continued through the jungle. Several spider monkeys were leaping about and shrieking high overhead in the trees they were walking by, playfully chasing their own tails or those tails of their companions. The boys peered anxiously from the ground. This, after all, was the first time they had seen wild creatures in their own habitat, uncaged. In the zoo, the animals were at the mercy of people. Here, people were at the mercy of the animals.

"They look very playful and harmless," Waikiki explained. "But up close, if they are cornered or upset, they can bite like dogs. They have very sharp teeth."

A half mile later they came to a small clearing where a herd of deep chestnut-red antelopes grazed. One of the largest of the antelopes remained alert, its narrow head held high, and its large ears perked in anticipation of danger. Upon seeing the company approaching, the animal wiggled its tail and fled, and the herd followed immediately behind. The herd vanished in a graceful running jump, as though it was performing a ballet.

On the other side of the clearing Simcha noticed what seemed at first to be a spotted leopard. He swallowed hard before he could get the words of warning out of his throat. "Leopard!" he shouted. "Look over there! A leopard!"

Again Waikiki calmed the boys and told them not to panic, for many animals resembled other animals from a distance. The small spotted animal in the brush across the clearing, he pointed out, was only an old hyena. Hyenas, he added, were in no rush to bother people. Sure enough, as they continued to walk in the direction of the hyena, it set off into the nearby thicket.

The group stopped where the hyena had stood and Waikiki pointed his rifle at the remains of a zebra. "Hyenas are known as cowards," he said, "they don't do their own hunting. They follow lions around and wait for them to do all the hard work. Then, after the lions have finished with their dinner, they move in and pick at the leftovers. Very little is wasted in the jungle. Man can learn a lot from the animals, eh?"

Simcha perked up. "The Talmud says that!"

"The what?" Waikiki asked in puzzlement. Moshe chuckled to himself. How, he wondered, was Simcha going to explain to

Waikiki about the Talmud? Simcha and his big mouth.

"Well," Simcha began, "the Talmud is... uh... well, it's... uh... the... uh... the books that contain my tradition. We're Jewish, see, and the Talmud explains what our tradition is all about and contains all of its basic laws, ethics and principles."

"Oh," Waikiki said, smiling. "Like the Bible."

"Not quite. See, the Bible is God's word; the outline, sort of. The... uh... the lesson plan. The Talmud is the filling-in of the outline, the ink that connects the dotted lines, the... uh... the details of how to practice the teachings of the Bible and how to apply them to the widest variety of situations and times," explained Simcha.

"Oh? I understand. And what does your Talmud teach about nature?"

"Like *you* said, Waikiki. We can learn everything from nature. We can learn to avoid laziness from the ant. We can learn modesty from the cat, and..."

"Begging your pardon," Waikiki interrupted swiftly, "I don't mean to be rude and interrupt your Talmudic teachings, but a very immodest cat is on his way toward us right now, and I think we should move on. He might want to finish what neither the lions nor the hyena could."

Simcha looked in the direction Waikiki was pointing his rifle and almost let out a shriek at the sight of the large, menacing leopard moving stealthily through the brush toward the clearing. The group moved quickly away from the zebra remains and continued into the jungle, in search of a place to set up camp before the sun set. Looking behind him, Moshe noticed that the leopard was hovering over the zebra's carcass while casting threatening glances at the safari party. "Looks like he's trying to decide on the menu," he said with a chuckle to Simcha. "Trying to choose between zebra left-overs or five fresh humans. Let's not tempt him."

The sun was setting, casting a flaming red and orange glow

across and between the distant trees. As night slowly fell, swarms of gnats and mosquitoes engulfed the campers, at times in swarms so thick the boys were afraid they would inhale them through their noses. More than once, Moshe had to pick one out of his ears or from the corners of his mouth. Simcha could hardly keep his eyes on the trail any longer, distractedly slapping his arms and neck in what he soon realized was a futile attempt to keep the tiny insects from biting him. Again the natives seemed unmoved by yet another attempt by nature to keep humans off her property. They walked nonchalantly on, speaking animatedly amongst themselves and frequently laughing, while armies of gnats and mosquitoes, speckled across their necks and faces, competed for their blood.

The boys were beginning to tire. It had been a long day of rough riding yesterday and this morning. And now they had to endure an even longer day of hard walking, weighed down by hiking and camping supplies, baked by the sun's unrelenting heat. The guides whispered what seemed to Simcha to be mocking remarks as to how the hike was certainly going to wear the boys out. They kept smiling as they ping-ponged their brief Swahili sentences, their eyes gazing sporadically at the panting youths. The trek was so intense that Simcha and Moshe had said nothing to one another for hours, channeling every ounce of their strength into propelling their bodies uphill toward what looked like a towering wall of concrete.

"Here we rest a little," Waikiki finally said, to the relief of the boys. "Because soon we climb this rock."

The boys chuckled as they guzzled from their canteens.

"We're too tired for jokes," Moshe mumbled back at Waikiki.

"No joke," Waikiki said. "We must climb the rocks and get to the other side if we are to make camp tonight. Unless you want to turn back and continue our safari by jeep."

The boys looked around them. Waikiki was right. There was no other way to go but over the towering wall of jagged rock.

To the left they spied a long, seemingly endless drop into thick brush; to the right, a slope that led to a hanging cliff and yet another drop into eternity. Behind them, the security of walkable trails leading back to Nairobi and the plush, air-conditioned hotel room they now so longed for. But the passion for adventure was stronger. After all, were they not Emes Junior Interpol, the crack detective team? They looked at one another with expressions of mutual agreement.

"We hear and obey," they said almost in unison, comically, evoking laughter in the bellies of the guides. Everyone helped tighten and reinforce each other's packs and braced themselves for the steep and dangerous climb. Waikiki and the other guides smiled defeatedly at one another, mumbling their disappointment at the boys' persistence. They had hoped they could induce them to call off the trek. After all, it had been a good two days already. How much more hiking would the boys want to do? Waikiki was sure that once they'd reached the 'end of the world,' where there was only a steep drop or a steep climb, the boys would agree they'd had enough. But Waikiki had misjudged the two slight boys.

As they were getting ready to climb, the other two guides whispered something to Waikiki that seemed to cause him alarm.

Simcha, noticing the change in Waikiki's face, asked, "Is there any problem?"

"Not really. You two are sure you want to go on? Sure you haven't had enough?"

"What's the problem?" Simcha repeated.

"My friends here are just saying that after we climb to the other side, we should just go a little further and then turn back."

"Why?" asked Moshe. "Is there a problem on the other side?"

"Uh... no, no problem. They are probably getting tired and just want to start turning back tomorrow, if that's okay."

The boys eyed each other. Something in Waikiki's tone of voice struck them as strange. He was definitely hiding something.

"Why can't you tell us what's going on? I thought this safari was supposed to last longer; that we could keep going for four days in each direction. That's what my father told us."

The guides began arguing with Waikiki in Swahili. Finally Waikiki looked at Simcha and Moshe with resignation.

"Okay, okay," he finally said, throwing his arms in the air. "Here's the truth. This route is not one we usually take on any four-day hike. We usually go in another direction. I thought since you were two young boys that I could cut the hiking time in half by tiring you out on this long walk, ending up here within two days as we did. I thought for sure that by the time we came to this area, which we call 'the end of the world,' you two would not only be tired, but scared, too, and certainly not in any mood to climb so high. So it was my idea to take you this way, and now they're angry at me for suggesting it because, as you see, it didn't work. You want to go on. I misjudged the two of you."

"I still don't understand why we can't go on for two more days, if we choose, in the direction we're going now. I mean, this isn't really where the world ends, Waikiki," insisted Moshe.

"Ah yes, that. You see, uh… our people do not prefer to venture beyond this point. This is why we call it 'the end of the world.' Not because we actually believe the world ends here, but we believe that *our* world ends here. That beyond this area, on the other side of this gigantic rock, is the world of the super-natural, a world that is forbidden to mankind. It's an old super-stition. Strange goings-on have been reported about the world beyond this area. They fill our tradition with awe and mystery. It is known as the forbidden world or the 'world of the gods.' So Jono and Nick are nervous. And I am nervous, too. Our people do not go beyond this area, never more than a few kilometers at the very most. So if you are insistent, we are willing to go just a bit beyond, but then we must turn back. You must promise them we will turn back or they will not want to con-tinue."

"What can we do?" asked Moshe helplessly. "We can't go anywhere without you guys, so whatever you say... As long as you are willing to take us back when we're done."

Simcha nodded in agreement. Waikiki smiled in relief and conveyed the boys' message to the other two, who broke out in sighs of relief and resumed their broad smiles and enthusiastic looks. The group prepared for the climb.

"Remember," Waikiki instructed the boys, "do not grip rocks and climb until you check out each and every rock. Make sure anything you grab is not at all loose, and is not moving—you know—like a snake. Same with your feet. Do not place your feet on any rock or branch before checking to make sure it is safe and can carry your weight. Also, do not look down as you climb. Just keep moving up. Push your bodies against the rock at all times. No stopping, just keep climbing."

Jono and Nick positioned themselves behind the boys for the sake of their safety, while Waikiki took the lead. Up the rock they went, stepping and grasping ever so carefully onto jagged formations of stone. At times they made convenient use of the protruding roots of mountain brush which grew sporadically along the way. Simcha watched Waikiki's every move, where he put his hands, where he placed his feet, how he lifted his tall, strong body, his weight always pressing against the stone wall. Similarly, Moshe observed Simcha's every move, but both felt reassured by the presence of the two experienced climbers immediately behind them.

Just when it seemed to Simcha that his aching legs would carry him no further, Waikiki announced the appearance of the summit. Panting heavily, their clothes drenched with sweat, the boys mustered their ebbing strength and climbed the last few yards to the top.

"Downhill from here," Waikiki laughed, breathing heavily and pointing to a downward sloping field of small trees and brush which led to a thick rain forest below. Far beyond the forest, Simcha and Moshe could see a long, winding river which disappeared further on, turning and twisting sharply into a very dense, mountainous jungle.

"Wow!" exclaimed Moshe at the awesome sight of the river cutting through the magnificent scenario. "Look at that!" The boys waited for Waikiki to tell them about the river as he had about everything else they had seen along the way, or at least inform them of its name. But Waikiki remained silent for a few moments, his eyes fixed on the distant river. It seemed that he and the two other guides were distracted by the far-away river and had all but forgotten the boys.

CHAPTER 5

A Hollywood Rescue Scene

Larry shrieked like a wildman as he swerved his brand new furnished van around a sharp bend along Highway 3. The scorching Ethiopian weather had gotten to him after three days of driving through the vast, deserted countryside, thousands of square miles of just parched land and desert. His wife Gloria, seated beside him, held her breath as they reached another sharp bend in the road, and Larry let out a yell of delight that outdid the first one.

"Larry!" she protested. "We're not in California. Please be careful. I mean, if we break down here we'll never find help. Take it easy. I'm nervous enough as it is."

"Hey sweets, don't you worry. Old Larry's the best darned driver G-d ever made. Here comes another! Hold on, sweets, this is a biggie! Wheeeeeee!"

The van swerved around a bend in the road flanked by large, hand-painted signs which read: "Danger! Sharp Curve! Maximum 20 K/H." Oblivious to the sign, Larry skidded the van around the curve, causing the speeding vehicle to spin completely around several times on two wheels. Gloria screamed louder than Larry this time and almost passed out. When the van finally came to a halt on all four wheels, Gloria swung open her door and jumped out, shouting.

"You're crazy! You're a maniac! That's what you are! A maniac! I don't know what's gotten into you, Larry! You could've gotten us killed!"

"Killed? Us?" Larry laughed as he jumped out of the van to join his wife at the side of the road. "Don't you remember what that rabbi once told us? You know that guy that gave that what-chamacallit session at Steve's place that Saturday. Torah session! That's it, the Torah session. Ain't that cute, hon'? Torah? Torah Torah Torah—pow! Hey sweets, don't be so upset. Nothing can kill two nice folks like us who came all the way out to Africa to do a what-did-he-call-it?"

"*Mitzvah.*"

"Yeah, that's right, sweets. A *mitzvah*. We're doing a *mitzvah*, sweets. Come on, sweets, let's do the *mitzvah* thing!"

Larry grabbed his wife's arms and began dancing on the highway, but Gloria moved along with him like a rag doll, not the least in the mood to dance with her tall, husky husband after he had almost ended their lives. "*Mitzvah! Mitzvah!*" he shouted as he danced wildly about, finally releasing his unwilling wife to dance by himself. "Torah Torah Torah! *Mitzvah Mitzvah Mitzvah!* Heydoodledidle, heydoodledidle! Whooopeeeeee! Whoooopeeeeee!"

Gloria sat down on a rock and held her head in her hands. She still couldn't believe she had actually gone off to Ethiopia with her crazy Larry. She missed the rolling green mountains of Mendocino County, back in California, and the cool roaring ocean that met them at towering cliffs adorned with majestic redwood trees. What was she doing in the ugly wilderness of a barren Ethiopia, stricken with drought and famine? How could she have let Larry talk her into coming with him to save Ethiopian Jews? She was no soldier. She was no commando. Let the Israelis handle it, she had told Larry and his friends again and again and again. But no, Larry and his even crazier buddies, David, Steve, Rubin, Noam, Jack, and Susie had voted her down. The efforts of the Israeli government were insufficient, they argued. They weren't enough and weren't doing the job fast enough. Israel was busy enough in Lebanon. In the meantime, thousands of Ethiopian Jews were trapped in a land that persecuted them, a land that starved them. Action was needed immediately and quickly to smuggle them out of Ethiopia. Now. Not tomorrow. Not next month. Not bit by bit. Human life was at stake.

"Sweets," said Larry, calming down from the wild dance. "Hey sweets, I'm sorry I freaked out, you know? Come on, sweets, don't look so sad."

"If you call me 'sweets' just one more time," said Gloria, lifting her head from her hands, "I'm going to..." her eyes met his and she paused. How could she be angry with the big lug, big Larry, with his long bushy red beard and balding head? He looked so innocent standing there, she thought. So crazy and innocent. He looked like a little boy who had gotten himself into a heap of trouble. Larry sure had done just that by volunteering for the mission. She hated him for it and she loved him for it. How many men would risk their lives for others? He couldn't read a word of Hebrew, never saw the inside of a synagogue in his life. She wasn't even sure he believed in G-d. But when it came to helping somebody out of trouble, anybody and any trouble, you could always count on Red Larry. She smiled. She laughed. Then she rose and gave him a tight hug. "You can call me 'sweets' any time and as often as you like, lug," she said.

When she noticed that Larry wasn't smiling back at her, or even returning her hug, she became concerned. Was he angry at her for bawling him out? After all, he did almost drive that van off the road and maybe even off the cliff. She stepped back, prepared for an argument. "Larry!" she started to scream, but not in anger anymore. Larry stared right through her. Something had happened to him. He looked drained and unsteady. He wasn't himself. He stood there, as if he were chained to the road. His eyes just gazed blankly ahead. He said nothing. She wiped the sweat off her brow, and then it occured to her that Larry wasn't sweating at all. A big man like him. In 100 degrees or more. Something was strange. She felt her heart pounding so hard it seemed like it was trying to break out of her rib cage.

"Larry?"

"Yes," he said weakly. Then he slumped down on the road. He slowly began to open his mouth, then coughed, then tried to swallow but couldn't. He bent his head between his legs. Larry, Gloria now realized, was dehydrated. Maybe he even had sunstroke. Immediately, she ran to the rear of the van and yanked the doors open, frightened, very frightened. What if she was too late? Larry was worse off than an overheated car. She pulled out a gallon jug of water and ran to him, pouring half of it over his head as she approached him. She then held his head back and poured some over his face and into his mouth.

Within moments Larry was better. He looked at her and simply said: "I almost drowned in the heat. I suddenly felt so weakened and dizzy. I had no idea I was dried out. I mean I felt okay. Like I know I acted a little crazy driving. But at the time I was doing it, like it felt okay. I felt okay... a little dizzy—but okay. And all the time I was dehydrated. My brain was probably going haywire, you know? Like plugging an air-conditioner into 120-wiring while the washer and dryer are on."

Gloria cupped her hand over his mouth. "If you keep rambling like this, you're gonna dry up again. Now how far are we from that refugee camp?"

"Huh? Oh yeah, refugee camp. Yeah, that's right, we're smuggling Jews. For a moment I thought we were in Death Valley, California. Yeah, right, we're in Ethiopia! Hello, Ethiopia! The refugee camp. We're about maybe 45 miles away. Could be 50. Depends on the heat."

The couple resumed their ride, this time with Gloria at the wheel. Larry sat beside her, thankful to be alive; thankful for the feel of the gallon jug on his lap and for the clear, tasteless, colorless liquid it contained. He drank continuously, ever-thirsty. He was thankful for the beads of perspiration which after a while began to form on his forehead and on his arms and back. "Thank G-d, I'm alive," he thought to himself. "It feels good to sweat again. Real good." Then, turning to Gloria, he said: "Hey sweets, we got any deodorant with us?"

She looked at him fondly and after a long pause said: "You never smelled better."

When they arrived at the turnoff which led to the refugee camp, Larry instructed his wife to pull the van over to the side. When she parked it, he withdrew some tools from the glove compartment and started unscrewing nuts and bolts from underneath the dashboard. "Sure this will work, Larry?" Gloria asked. She knew it would. After all, it was her idea. But she was growing increasingly nervous about the mission, now that they were minutes away from it.

"Sure. I think it's great. We got a good half tank of gas left, but by fooling around with the gas gage here it'll show up as 'empty' on the dashboard indicator. We'll act like a couple of crazy, unsuspecting tourists looking for a gas station. They'll see the indicator on 'empty' and believe us, and..."

"Yes, and then what, Larry?"

"Well, something will work out, and we can smuggle out those twenty-seven Ethiopian Jews. I mean, don't worry, sweets, they know we're coming. That Israeli fella, what's his name..."

"Tamari?"

"Yeah, Tamari, Tamari. Anyway, he told us he's gotten word to the group that we're coming in a van, two irate tourists out of gas, you know. So they'll do the rest. They'll sneak into the van their own way. All we gotta do is keep everybody busy, you know? Make a commotion or something."

"Is this the last trip we have to make, or do we have to do more? I mean, you haven't given me a straight answer about this yet. All you say is maybe, you'll see, you don't know. What is it?"

"Well, like I once explained, we're each doing different regions. Tamari and his gang are doing their area, right? Okay. Then there's Noam and Susie, way on the other side, near Odi Addad, doing the refugee camp over there. Then Jack and David, going through what's left of the Jewish villages out east. And Steve is with Rubin, hitting the mountain country, where the Ethiopian Jews are reportedly fleeing on foot to G-d-knows-where. So there ought to be about a thousand or more, according to Tamari, this trip around. He said we only need to get these twenty-seven people out of this camp. Unless the others fail to get their people out, we're done after this. Mission accomplished. We can go to..."

"Morocco and celebrate," Gloria finished. "I'll be so relieved when this is over, Larry, that I won't mind just going back to California and celebrating over some ice-cold American lemonade."

"All set. The gage is all messed up now."

Larry took the driver's seat and drove the van off the road, up an unpaved road leading to the camp. As the van sped up the road, a cloud of sand whirled about it, some of it blowing into the car and all over the couple. "Larry! Slow down! The sand's blowing in!"

"That's the idea. We have to look really ragged and desperate, sweets."

After twenty minutes of flying through whirlwinds of sand and rocks, the van came to an abrupt halt. As the sand subsided the couple saw the outline of barbed-wire fencing. They had arrived. Behind the fence hundreds of tents were set up where many Ethiopians fleeing the famine and drought were now settled temporarily for relief. Larry backed up the van a few yards while Gloria scanned the area looking for an entrance.

Suddenly they heard the rumbling sounds of approaching jeeps. Gloria grabbed her husband's hand and held it tight. The jeeps stopped a few inches in front of the van, and six soldiers jumped out, their automatic weapons poised. Other soldiers remained in the jeeps, aiming their Kalatchnikov assault rifles at the van. An officer approached Larry's side of the van while a soldier kept his eyes on Gloria.

"English?" the officer asked briskly. "French? American?"

"Uh... American!" shouted Larry, acting scared or being scared. He couldn't figure out which it was. Gloria swallowed hard and then mustered all her emotional strength and started the act. "Larry!" she screamed. "What do they want? Who are they? Is this a gas station, Larry?"

"Don't worry so much!" Larry yelled back, acting along with her. The two suddenly found themselves swept up in their own act. It wasn't as hard as they had thought it would be. In fact, it was nearly fun. The officer jumped back as the two started shouting nervously at one another, acting oblivious to the guns pointed at them.

"Look what you've done!" Gloria shouted.

"What I've done?! This was *your* idea. You're the one who said, 'Go down this road, honey,'" he mimicked, "'Go up that road. Turn here. And turn there. Maybe there's a gas station there, maybe up that road.'"

"Stop making fun of me! You're the fool, not me! Why didn't you fill the tank like I suggested you do before we left the city?! You always do that! You always leave everything for later! You're so impatient! Always in a hurry! 'We'll fill up later,'" she now mimicked. "'There's bound to be plenty of gas stations along the way. I just want to get on the road already.'"

"Oh yeah? Well, let me tell you something..."

The officer was growing impatient and tried to interrupt.

"Excuse me, please. My English not good, but you need gas?

We help you. First show me passport, please."

Larry started rummaging through the glove compartment. He knew that Gloria had the passports in the knapsack by her feet, but he was going to play this to the end. "Where are the passports?" he shouted at Gloria.

"They're in the knapsack, you jerk!"

"Can't you leave anything where I put it?" he yelled. "I put them in the glove compartment, and then you take them out and throw them in the knapsack! I don't understand why you can't ever leave things alone!"

"That's right! Leave them in the glove compartment, eh? Is that what you wanted? What if someone stuck their head in the window while we were parked somewhere and took our passports, eh?"

"Well, we'd have locked the doors."

"Oh yeah? And the windows would have been shut? And the heat would have built up and we would have returned to an oven! Isn't it much simpler to take them with us wherever we go? What's wrong with you?"

"What's wrong with *me*? What's wrong with *you*? Why didn't you tell me you put the passports in the knapsack? Eh? What if I was driving alone somewhere and got stopped and then had to look through the glove compartment for a passport that wasn't there, eh? What then?"

The officer was growing a little nervous.

"Excuse, please, but we help you with the gas. You follow us, yes? But please, let me see passport. Ordinary procedure," the officer said, managing a small smile.

Gloria reached into the knapsack and withdrew their passports. The officer examined them and returned them cordially. He then jumped back into his jeep and waved to the other soldiers to move on. Larry turned the ignition key in a way that made the van sound like it was having a difficult time starting. "He didn't even check my gage," Larry complained in a whisper. Gloria smiled at him and replied: "He was so taken by our dramatic argument that he needed no further proof. As far as he's concerned, we're out of gas and he's out of patience. And we're also out of our heads." Larry pulled the van up behind the jeeps and followed them into the compound, passing several armed guard towers and hundreds of curious faces.

"Where do you think the Jews are?" Gloria asked. "I mean, this place is huge. Where are we going to pick them up?"

"Gloria, they'll spot us a mile away. That's what's so great about this van. It's so colorful, real loud colors. I knew it would come in handy. I mean, I'm sure that when they spot this crazy van riding around they ain't gonna think it's an army truck, so don't worry."

"I am worried."

"So am I. But what should I do? Jump atop the van and make an announcement? 'All African Jews interested in being smuggled out of this terrible country, please enter the van immediately!'"

"Keep it down, Larry. The soldiers might hear you."

The van came to a stop behind the officer's jeep. The officer got out of the jeep and walked over to Larry again. "You wait here, please. My men bring you gasoline."

When they were alone again, they climbed out of the van and together leaned against it, surveying the thousands of huts and refugees. Gloria suddenly gasped. *"Oy gevalt!"* she sighed.

"Gee, I didn't know you knew Hebrew," said Larry, looking at Gloria in surprise.

"It's Yiddish, Larry. It means "oh, help!" I just thought of something awful."

"What now? Did we forget toothpaste? Extra shoelaces?"

"No, worse. Our trick won't work if they put too much gas in our tank. Know what I mean? They think the tank is empty," whispered Gloria, her eyes filled with worry.

"No problem. We go by the gage. It's broken, right? It's

giving us the wrong information. Don't worry, sweets. It'll be okay." Then Larry remembered something and grinned warmly at Gloria. "You're forgetting we have a reserve tank on this rig! We'll have them pour the gas into that. They won't know the difference."

"Is the reserve tank empty?"

"Yeah, I forgot to fill it."

"My hero. For once, your lousy memory worked in our favor," Gloria said, leaning over and kissing him on the cheek.

By this time, twilight had arrived and the hot air was gradually becoming replaced by a cool gust sweeping across the desert. Two soldiers arrived by jeep, leading a fuel truck covered with military camouflage. The troops connected the fuel hose to the reserve tank of the van under Larry's direction while Gloria kept her eyes busy looking for the twenty-seven Jewish refugees. In the distance, huddled together, she noticed a group of people in robes: men, women, and children. There was something different about them, she felt. Maybe it was them. It was difficult to tell.

One of the members of the huddle, a tall, lanky, bearded man, started towards her, eyeing her suspiciously. He approached her closely and then detoured around the van, as if heading somewhere else. He kept walking straight ahead, now oblivious to the van and its strange owners. After the tank had been filled, Gloria noticed him again, walking back to the huddle even farther from the van than before. Maybe he was checking out the van. Maybe he wanted to make sure. But now what? The tank was filled, and she and Larry could be ready to get back on the road again.

"How are we going to get the refugees on board?" asked Gloria in a nervous whisper. "Tamari told us to try to stall and stay overnight," she reminded Larry.

"I know. I know. I hope we can do it. I think we need to start with Act Two," Larry proposed.

"Okay, here goes."

Gloria sat down on the ground and dropped her head between her knees. Larry ran over and knelt beside her. "Gloria, are you okay? What's wrong?"

"I can't travel anymore today, Larry. I'm sick. I'm so dizzy, tired and sick. Can't we stay here overnight and sleep in the van?"

"Are you nuts? I want to get back on the road. We'll go to the next city and find a decent hotel! I can't sleep in the van! Come on, Gloria, stop acting like such a baby."

"How dare you!" yelled Gloria. The soldiers were growing agitated again and summoned the officer over the radio. It wasn't long before he arrived in a speeding jeep. He hurried over to Larry, who hovered over his wife, shouting.

"Excuse me, please," the officer pleaded. "This is military land. You must leave now. You must pay thirty American dollars for the gasoline, and then you must go."

"Thirty dollars?!" Larry yelled, now turning to the officer. Larry's tall and husky frame intimidated the man, but he quickly regained his composure.

"Yes. We help you. You need gas. This is not gas station. You pay thirty dollars and go."

Larry reached into his pocket for his wallet.

"I can't go!" Gloria cried. "Can't you tell him to let us stay? I can't travel anymore!"

"My wife isn't feeling well. If it was up to me, officer, I'd just get out of here right now. I'd rather be in a hotel. But I've tried arguing with her, and I'm not getting anywhere. Maybe one of your soldiers should fire some warning shots at her or something."

The officer took the money from Larry's hand and pocketed it. He looked at Gloria and then at Larry. "We cannot let you stay. This is property of government. You must leave. I am sorry your wife sick, but you must leave now."

"But my wife is sick! What do you want me to do? Throw her into the van like a dead animal?"

"I am sorry. I understand. But I take big risk if I let you stay."

Larry reached for his wallet again.

"What if I make it worth the risk?"

"Fifty American dollars," the officer said, smiling at the wad of bills.

"Forty."

"Forty-five."

"Sold."

"But in the morning you go. Before day. Okay?"

"We'll be long gone by daybreak. I promise you that."

The officer took the money and saluted Larry. The soldiers left, and Larry and Gloria climbed into the furnished van to start dinner, which meant opening cans of tuna, peas, and carrots. The two dined into the night, wondering and worrying about exactly who the black Jews were and how they were going to locate them. While they were still talking animatedly to one another, there was a quiet knock on the door. Gloria looked out of the van window to see who it was, but it was too dark to see anything.

"It's probably them!" whispered Larry, his eyes shining with excitement. "Just open the door! Quickly!"

Gloria opened the door, and two small girls crawled up into the van. Gloria looked past them to see whether there was anyone else. To her surprise, there was no one. "Uh, come on in," she said to the girls. Then she remembered that she didn't know their language. The girls appeared frightened, their eyes so wide open they made Larry think of automobile headlights. "Where are their parents? And everybody else?" he whispered. "What's happening, Gloria?"

Gloria looked out again, straining her eyes for any signs of movement in the night. A giant floodlight rotated around the camp from high above a guard tower in the camp's center. Gloria followed the light, hoping to discover some more Jewish refugees approaching the van, but there were none. Just the girls. She clumsily attempted to communicate to them, wanting to display her concern for their plight, but she couldn't find the right gestures. Finally, she offered them a paper plate with some tuna fish, which they eagerly ate without making a sound. Larry poured them some apple juice, which they guzzled down as if they hadn't had anything to drink in days.

After fifteen very long and nerve-wracking minutes, there was another soft knock on the van door. Gloria again pushed past their equipment to the door and peered out the window into the faces of a man and a woman. She opened the door quickly, and they practically leaped into the van and embraced the two girls. "Maybe they're coming in twos," whispered Larry as he poured some juice for the couple. "That's smart. I guess they'd be spotted in no time if they all came at once. That's pretty smart. Pretty smart. We're gonna have us some party here, eh Gloria?"

"Please, Larry," Gloria pleaded, "you're making me nervous. I just want to get out of here."

"Take it easy, sweets. We can't just pull out in the middle of the night. We've got about four more hours until dawn. If we leave any sooner than that they'll get mighty suspicious, don't you think?"

"I guess. But how are we going to spend four hours cooped up in here with twenty-seven people?"

"Hey, come on, you're forgetting. This ain't no sleepaway camp. This is a mission. This is war. We're not here on a picnic or camping trip. Save that for home."

They were interrupted by three soft knocks on the rear door. Gloria opened the door and greeted an extremely thin young man escorting an elderly woman. Larry went over to help lift the frail woman onto the van. This went on for close to an hour and a half, until the van was filled almost to capacity. Some of the Ethiopians were lying down on the floor, some on the van's pull-out sofa bed. Others sat up against the walls of the van, while yet others found comfortable positions by lying half on the floor, half on their friends or relatives. Larry and Gloria moved to the front of the van and tried to catch some sleep in their seats.

About daybreak, Larry finally began drifting off, snoring slightly, which brought muffled giggles from the children in the rear of the van. Gloria had been asleep for two hours, but was awakened by the giggling. She was glad to find Larry asleep. He sure needed it. He was usually so robust, but yesterday's fainting spell had probably taken its toll on him. Looking out the window, Gloria suddenly noticed the rising sun making its appearance from behind distant mountains, slowly but surely. She gently patted Larry on the shoulder, trying to wake him up. "Larry," she whispered. "Larry. It's time to get out of here. Larry. Larry."

Larry was totally out, she realized. He could sleep through anything. Without further thought, she climbed out of the van and walked around to Larry's side. Then, with all her might, she maneuvered him into the passenger seat and took his place at the wheel. He muttered something in his sleep and then snored even louder, his head virtually hanging out the window and his legs sprawled limply over the floor. Gloria turned to the back and motioned with her hands to the refugees that they had to hide. This time they understood her gestures and covered themselves with the blankets she had provided. Some concealed themselves inside of cabinets, closets, the sofa bed. Gloria checked every window. All were drawn shut, and the van started to move.

As the van passed the guard post, the soldier on duty smiled at the comical sight of Larry's sleeping head hanging out the window, snoring. He saluted Gloria and opened the gate for her. The van pulled out in a cloud of dust and headed toward the main road. The farther she drove from the compound, the more relieved she felt and the easier she breathed. It somehow felt as if she had not been breathing at all until now, she thought. Her forehead rained perspiration as she nervously approached the main highway. She knew that if any patrol should catch her turning off the camp road onto the highway, they would surely stop her and want to know what she was doing at the refugee camp or on a government road. And that meant they would want to inspect the van.

The van swerved off the dirt road onto Highway 3 again, its tires screeching chillingly as Gloria floored the gas pedal. The van raced off like a jet on a runway. Boy, was she glad to get back on the highway again. She was even gladder that the road was empty when she got there. But she suddenly became aware of a steady whirring sound. She looked out the window and to her shock saw a helicopter hovering high above her to the left.

"Larry!" she yelled in terror. "Larry, wake up! Larry, we're being followed!"

Larry mumbled, then cleared his throat and rubbed his tired eyes.

"What is it, Gloria? Where are we?" he murmured, as he slowly pulled himself upright in his seat. "Where am I? Where's the steering wheel?"

"Larry, you're in my seat. We're on the highway. We made it to the highway, but now we're being followed."

"What? Where?" Larry exclaimed, looking into the rear-view mirror and seeing nothing but a deserted stretch of highway.

"Not on the road, Larry, up there! Look up there! Above us!"

Larry stuck his head out the window and looked into the pink dawn sky at the military helicopter slowly descending toward them. "Oh my God!" he said. "Oh my God! Gloria, did you turn right or left when you got to the highway?"

"I turned right. What difference does it make?" she cried in annoyance.

"If you'd have turned left, we'd be in a lot of trouble." Larry was now looking out of the window, trying to guess from the desolate landscape where they were.

"I don't understand. Can't helicopters fly to the right? How does my going right solve anything? He's still up there?" asked a trembling Gloria.

"Calm down. You don't understand. Tamari told us about a tunnel, remember? He said in case we're discovered or followed to stop in the tunnel."

"What tunnel?"

Just as she said this, the van approached a sharp curve and at the turn of the bend Gloria noticed a not-too-distant tunnel which cut through a mountain. As they neared the tunnel they heard a roaring voice from the helicopter's loudspeaker speaking in English: "Stop! Please stop at the side of the road!"

Gloria pulled the van into the dark tunnel and slowed down. "Okay, Larry, we're in the tunnel. Now what?"

"Beats me. Tamari just said stop in the tunnel if we're followed."

"Larry, I'm so scared I'm going to die! We can't just sit here. They'll land that helicopter somewhere and come in here and shoot us."

"Tamari said..." Larry repeated, but was interrupted by the touch of somebody's hand on his arm through the van window. Startled, Larry turned around and met the eyes of Yossi, Tamari's lieutenant. "*Shalom,* How are you? Tamari sends his regards," Yossi said, smiling. At the same time, the doors of the van were swung wide open and, to the couple's surprise, a canvas-covered truck backed out of nowhere, and their passengers scrambled into it, slamming the doors of the van behind them.

"Your mission is over, my friends," Yossi said, still smiling coolly. "We take it from here. See you in Nairobi in about a week. We'll celebrate, yes? Now you must leave the tunnel immediately. Tell them you slowed down, even stopped completely in the tunnel because it was so dark. You know, it was too sudden, the change from light to darkness. *Shalom, chaverim,*[1] and *l'hitraot*[2]!"

Gloria breathed a sigh of relief and floored the gas pedal, heading for the other side of the tunnel. "What was that last thing he said?" she asked.

"Oh, something in French and English. I think it was 'La hit the road.'"

At the other end of the tunnel they saw the helicopter in the process of landing, its gigantic blades whirling streams of dust into the air. Several soldiers leaped out, rifles held over their heads, and positioned themselves on the road to block the van. Gloria stopped the van and waited for an officer to approach.

"We are sorry," he said. "But we must to check."

"What's wrong?" Gloria asked. "Were we speeding, or something?"

"I told you not to drive so fast!" Larry yelled, starting up his act again. Gloria caught on and responded by turning at him like a wild cat.

"Don't you criticize my driving!" she yelled loudly, shocking the officer. "If you don't like the way I drive, then why don't you drive it yourself? You lazy..."

"Please, madam," the officer pleaded. "We have no time. We must to check. Please."

"Check what?" Larry asked. "Our passports?"

"No. We get radio message about you. Your passport is not problem. But maybe you take some refugees with you in your van, no? We to check.

"Refugees?" Gloria exclaimed. "In *our* van?" Then, turning to Larry, she started screaming again. "Did you sneak some refugees into our van without telling me anything about it?"

[1]*chaverim*—friends [Hebrew].
[2]*l'hitraot*—see you soon [Hebrew].

"What for? Why would I be sneaking refugees around? What are you, nuts?"

The officer kept his eyes on the seemingly crazy American couple while four soldiers ran to the rear of the van and yanked the doors open, their rifles cocked. They shouted their disappointing findings to the officer, who seemed to find it impossible to believe. He ran to the rear of the van and peered inside. Sure enough, there was no one. He climbed inside and inspected the cabinets, the sofa bed, the closet. Nothing.

"Oh my G-d!" Larry whispered.

"You've really been getting very religious lately, Larry," Gloria said. "You're always saying 'Oh, my G-d!'"

"Oh my G-d!" Larry repeated, groaning loudly.

"What's wrong?"

"The plastic cups and paper plates. We gave those people food and drink last night. They're going to wonder what twenty-nine cups and plates are doing back there, each stained with apple juice and tuna fish."

Gloria swallowed hard and began to tremble. "Oh my G-d!" she said.

The officer appeared at Larry's side of the van and saluted.

"I apologize for inconvenience. You may go now. We are very sorry. A mistake. Have a good journey. Enjoy our mountains." He then waved at his troops and they scrambled back into the helicopter, which promptly rose back into the sky.

As the couple drove on down the highway, neither spoke. They were unsettled by what had almost happened and were trying to figure out why the officer did not question them about the cups and plates. Was he playing with them? Was he just pretending not to know? What was going on? Gloria pulled the van over to the side of the road. Almost instantaneously, the couple moved away the partition separating the front of the van from the furnished rear. To their amazement, the van was spotless. Not a single empty cup or used plate was to be seen. Israeli

Intelligence hadn't overlooked a thing. Not a thing.

***

Back on the canvas-covered truck, a jubilant Colonel Tamari was slapping the backs and shaking the hands of his aides to express his gratitude and congratulations. His leading guide, the traitor Samoa, was uncomfortable with the vociferous celebrating. Perspiring nervously, he saluted Tamari in the reserved, military way. "'D' zone," he thought, "'D' zone. Just get this truck to 'D' zone..."

CHAPTER 6
Lost in Africa

Moshe awoke from his deep sleep and started to scratch his chest. It itched terribly. As he scratched he felt a small lump underneath his shirt. It felt unusual for a mere mosquito bite, he thought. It felt very hard, like it wasn't even part of his skin. A little frightened, he sat up and began to unbutton his shirt. The campfire had long been extinguished by the gusty night winds, and everyone was fast asleep. Moshe switched on his flashlight and pointed it toward his chest, revealing a small black tick fastened to his skin and a red mark all around the area of his chest where the bug was feasting. Shivering at the sight of a tick sucking his blood, Moshe wasted no time trying to remove it. But unlike ordinary bugs, this one wouldn't budge, no matter how many times he slapped his chest.

Waikiki heard the commotion Moshe was making and got up to see what was going on. After all, who could sleep with the sounds of someone beating their chest? Simcha, too, woke up, but was too tired to move. He just lay there, wide eyed, observing what was happening. Waikiki pulled a tweezer from his belt pouch and carefully extracted the tick from Moshe's chest. "Couldn't I just scratch it off?" Moshe asked.

"No. Then you would kill him and only scratch part of him off. Part of him would remain in your skin. You must remove the entire body at once. See?"

Waikiki held the tick up so Moshe could see it. Then he rummaged through his backpack until he found a plastic container of alcohol. He instructed Moshe to rub his chest with the alcohol to prevent infection. The other two guides lay wide awake in their sleeping bags. They had been awake for much of the night, growing more fearful by the minute about their close proximity to the forbidden region of 'the end of the world.' Waikiki, although anxious about any further hiking, was calm and had slept well. He now found it difficult to fall back asleep. As he lay down again, his mind filled with the terrifying stories his parents had told him as a child, stories of people venturing into the forbidden hills and never returning. He twisted and turned as he tried in vain to rid his mind of his fantasies. As for the boys, they were once again fast asleep.

A sudden boom of explosive thunder shook the earth as violent flashes of lightning pierced the jungle and lit up the night with a brightness almost greater than daylight. Waikiki and the other guides, panic-stricken, leaped to their feet and began screaming to one another in Swahili. A second clap of thunder nearly knocked them off their feet, and its accompanying lightning sent a tree crashing to the ground nearby. "We must go now!" Waikiki yelled at the boys who now sat bewildered in their sleeping bags. Simcha had never seen Waikiki act so scared. He seemed more educated and cultured than the others, unafraid of the superstitious tales of his people. But now he was as frightened as they were.

"It's only a rain storm," Moshe assured the guides. But the Kenyans, Waikiki included, were totally oblivious to the boys at this point, so badly frightened that nothing mattered anymore, and it was every man—and boy—for himself. They were still collecting their gear when a third blast of lightning cut through the nearby trees, followed by a roar of thunder that lasted for what seemed like almost a full minute, echoing across the mountains and shaking the earth. The guides were now so distraught that they dropped their equipment and ran off into the night, fearing that the gods were angry at their intrusion into the forbidden region.

The boys remained behind, collecting their gear, at first unaware that their guides had fled. It took several minutes before Simcha noticed that they had been abandoned. Torrents of rain poured down like needles, drenching them as they half-dragged, half-carried their supplies to a cleft underneath a huge boulder. They huddled close together in the narrow shelter and watched the storm rage through the jungle, each recalling a similar storm not long ago over the Galilee.

"Did they really leave us behind?" Moshe asked, a little fearfully.

"Are you kidding?" replied Simcha. "Of course not. They'd never do a think like that no matter what. Especially not Waikiki. They just ran for cover somewhere and probably thought we were right behind them. They'll be back out when the storm subsides. Don't worry."

"I'm not so sure about that, Simcha. They looked awfully scared to me. Really scared. They wanted to get out of this place fast," Moshe said pessimistically.

"Moshe, be reasonable. Do you really think that our safari guides, who are prepared to defend us against lions, would run out on us because of a storm?"

"It's not the storm, Simcha. You know that. It's the legends about this whole area. They believe in all that superstitious stuff, you know, 'the end of the world' and all that. To them their legends are real and more frightening than lions. They may be skilled and capable of overpowering wild animals, but they feel powerless and vulnerable before their spirits or gods."

"I sure hope you're wrong, Moshe," Simcha said, the thought of he and Moshe finding their way alone through the jungle sending a shiver down his spine. "If they don't return, we're lost. And, you know, I feel sorry for them. Imagine being raised believing in a bunch of lunatic gods. We're lucky that our under-standing of G-d is so totally different, that G-d is one and com-passionate."

"Yeah, but we have similar tendencies in Judaism too, don't we?"

"What do you mean, Moshe?"

"Well, aren't we always taught to fear G-d?"

"Wrong. It doesn't mean we're supposed to go through life being *afraid* of G-d, but in awe of G-d, aware of G-d."

"What do you mean? I thought it was 'fear of G-d.'"

"The Hebrew word for 'fear of G-d' is *yir'ah,* which also means sight, seeing. Remember yesterday when you saw that gigantic slab of rock towering into the sky, overlooking the mag-nificent scenery of mountains and that winding river in the dis-tance? Remember? What did you feel then?"

"I felt... uh... like saying 'wow!' I felt... like you put it, awed."

"Were you afraid?"

"In a way, but not in a bad way, not in the way that I would be afraid of a hungry lion jumping at me from a tree."

"Exactly, Moshe. See how there are different kinds of feelings that we call 'fear'? Well, the Torah speaks of 'fear of G-d,' it isn't telling us to be scared, but to be awed. And you can't become awed by something you can't see. So the more you learn about G-d, and the more you see and appreciate G-d's creations, the more awed you are. The more you say 'wow,' the more aware you become of G-d and G-d's goodness and day-to-day involve-ment with your needs."

"Wow! I never looked at it that way. Awesome. So we don't

have to be afraid of G-d after all!" Moshe was impressed with Simchas's explanation.

"On the contrary, we aren't supposed to be afraid of anything. Our bodies might react to danger. That's good. It's good to be afraid of fire, for example; otherwise we wouldn't recognize the danger it poses, and we could easily get hurt through carelessness. So we have this built-in system of fear for our protection. But why should we be afraid of what's good for us? That would be a wrong interpretation of our basic value system, a misuse of it. And we do that often."

"Oh, I get it," Moshe said, looking at Simcha gratefully. "You know, Simcha, I really want to tell you now how I much appreciate all the things you've taught me. You've been in yeshiva nearly all your life. I've only just begun. When I met you a few years ago I was totally ignorant. Since I joined you in yeshiva last year I've learned so much. But sometimes I think I'll never catch up with you!" Moshe paused in thought and then suddenly remembered that he was stuck in the middle of the African jungle without a guide. "Getting back to earth... we're in big trouble. I don't see Waikiki or either of the others. Not even a bird call from the other side of the rock. You'd at least think they'd try to call out at us. Look at the sky. I think the storm has subsided. It's hardly drizzling anymore. I don't even hear anymore thunder. Where are they? What are we going to do?"

"Well, let's try to get to them. I bet they'll be waiting for us, probably fast asleep after the ordeal they went through."

The boys crawled out of the tiny shelter and slung their packs over their shoulders. They walked through the brush a bit until they reached the steep slope. This side of the rock was less difficult to climb than the other side, as there were more rocky steps to scale and many more protruding roots and brush to hang onto. They approached the base of the boulder and prepared to scale it. Suddenly Simcha's eyes met with the bright green eyes of a black leopard nestled in a tree. Not a second later, Moshe had also spotted the leopard. Terrifed, they slowly backed away from the tree, hoping to re-start their climb somewhere else, but the leopard, having spotted its breakfast, had other plans for the boys.

Before they could lift a foot onto the first rock, the leopard had jumped to the ground and was walking in a hurried, steady way toward them. The boys had little choice but to run the other way now, away from the rock. The leopard increased its pace, but did not break into a run. The boys ran as fast as their legs could carry them, even deeper into the jungle. They ran in silence, for neither had a plan. All Moshe could think of was the immediacy of the threat and, ironically, how much the awe of G-d differs from the fear of a hungry black leopard.

Soon they were enveloped by the jungle. The wild sounds of birds mingled with the heavy thumping of the boys' hearts. They ran through the wet jungle blindly. Simcha dropped his heavy knapsack so he could run faster. Behind them they heard the leopard begin to growl, an indication, Simcha assumed, that it was about to make the fatal pounce on one of them. Yet the leopard seemed unsure of its quarry, since it never broke into a real run. The boys arrived at a steep grassy slope which seemed to lead down toward the river they had seen the day before from the summit of the rock. As carefully as they could manage, they half-ran, half-slid down the muddy slope into deeper brush, scratching their arms and legs as they fled their snarling pursuer. When they reached the bottom, they turned around briefly to see if the leopard was gaining. To their astonishment and relief, the animal had turned back up the slope.

Out of breath, with bruises and scratches all over their bodies, the boys continued walking briskly a little further, all the while keeping their eyes on the slope. Could the leopard really have gone for good? In gasping breaths Simcha whispered a prayer. Not far from the slope he sighted a large tree with a huge trunk. Perfect to lean against. Together he and Moshe slumped beneath it, still keeping their eyes pinned on the slope.

"It's too bad I don't jog," Simcha laughed, still out of breath.

Moshe began to laugh hysterically. He had been so scared. He had been convinced the leopard would catch them. All the leopard had to do was break into a run and one of them would have been forced to wrestle with it. Moshe closed his eyes and said a silent prayer. He wiped his forehead with his sleeve. He was covered in perspiration and his clothes were soaking from the drizzle. He felt as though he would never move his legs again. They were aching from yesterday's climb and now they were all scratched. He turned to Simcha, who was hopelessly trying to get mud off his jeans.

"Well, that was fun! What do you think we'll have for an encore? Poisonous snakes? Lions? Man-eating gorillas? I'm ready for anything," Moshe said, a menacing look on his face as he wildly threw punches at imaginary enemies. He then broke into a wide smile and lightly punched Simcha. "I bet you just set up this scene to illustrate your theory on fear!"

Simcha chuckled. "Right, I had this all planned out. I had Waikiki dress up as a leopard, just to teach you the difference between fear and awe. I just ran with you to get the exercise!" Simcha snorted to himself. "Sure, some sense of humor!"

Moshe suddenly became serious. "Well, in any case, I *do* know what you mean about fear! And it just struck me, Simcha, that it's absurd to fear G-d. I mean, the natural thing is to run away from something you fear, like we just did from that leopard. Yet we're supposed to be trying to get closer to G-d—not more distant! Being afraid of G-d will only make us want to run away, like those guides ran away."

Simcha nodded in full agreement on everything Moshe said. But he was preoccupied with a different problem. "Wonder what suddenly changed that leopard's mind about the menu?"

"Beats me. Think he saw something down here that we don't know about? Cats have good eyes, you know."

"I'm not sure. I know he didn't run off because of some superstitious fears! He must have seen or heard something down here that we didn't."

Moshe anxiously looked around and then up the tree against which they were leaning. His eyes opened wider than they ever had before, and wordlessly he rose and stepped back several paces from the tree against which Simcha was still sitting. "Simcha, don't move. I think I know what that leopard saw," Moshe said trembling.

Wrapped around a branch barely five feet above Simcha was an almost fifteen foot long pale brown snake, undoubtedly a boa constrictor. The snake slid slowly and cautiously down the branch toward Simcha. "What is it?" he nervously asked Moshe. "What's the matter?"

Moshe bit his lip and in a breathy, scared voice answered: "It's the biggest, longest snake I've ever seen in my life."

"The biggest, longest snake you've ever seen is on this tree, and you're telling me *not* to move?" Simcha cried, his eyes nearly popping out of their sockets.

"Well, maybe you should move. I don't know. Maybe it's better not to move and..."

Before Moshe could finish his sentence, Simcha made a sudden movement away from the tree and ran to where Moshe was standing. The two quickly moved further from the tree and observed the long reptile hiss as it slithered down the tree trunk. Suddenly it seemed to change its mind and jerked its head upward, coiling up the tree again. The boys were puzzled. First the leopard had turned back and now, just as suddenly, the snake made a U-turn. It just didn't make any sense...unless there was an even more dangerous animal lurking nearby.

The boys looked around suspiciously, but they didn't detect any movement amidst the rich green foliage. Only an exotic melange of insects busily scurrying across the thick layer of leaf mold on the ground.

What's going on?'' asked Moshe, as he watched the snake disappear up the vine-covered tree. He turned to Simcha, who was nervously biting his nails, his face pale and scared. "I'm getting the creeps."

"Just *you're* getting the creeps? How do you think I feel? I think I'm more scared not knowing what I'm scared of than I was being chased by a leopard or a boa constrictor! At least I could *see* them!"

"Let's get out of here! Something is going on. First the leopard takes off and now the snake. It's getting weird out here, Simcha. And I'm not in the mood to wait for any more surprises!"

Simcha gulped loudly. "Well... I think we're in for another surprise, Moshe. Look!" Simcha pointed to the slope on which they had fled the leopard. It was now covered with a moving dark red carpet.

For a few minutes Moshe looked toward the slope, not realizing what he was seeing.

"Come on, Moshe! Don't just stand there!"

The boys quickly took off further into the jungle. The mysterious pursuer was not a lion, a pack of wild dogs, or a crazed herd of elephants. In hot though mindless pursuit was a moving carpet of red ants; large, ugly, destructive ants capable of picking clean the carcass of any creature they cared to overtake. No living animal could hold off these ants, which had been driven by the preceding rainstorm. What could the piercing horns of an antelope or the sharp claws and teeth of a lion accomplish against such a nemesis? The tiny, six-legged soldiers swarmed across the floor of the jungle, heading toward the river and, in the process, forcing the boys to run in the same direction.

"I can't take too much more of this!" Moshe cried as they ran. "I mean it's been one thing after another since that storm. It's beginning to feel like the ten plagues in Egypt!"

"Take it easy, Moshe. You're not beginning to believe what those guides did, are you? You don't think there's a connection between all of this and our being in the forbidden zone?"

"Me? Of course not. I'm not superstitious. I don't believe in any of that stuff, believe you me. I'm sure it's just a result of the storm," said Moshe, almost as if he were trying to convince himself.

Soon they arrived at the bank of the mysterious river that Waikiki had neglected to identify. Looking behind them, they noticed the red blanket of ants flowing steadily in the distance, sending animals in flight and even frightening the bright, colorful birds into the clear morning sky.

"What are we going to do?" asked Moshe, desperately facing the raging river and then turning to observe the approaching red army at his back.

Simcha's face was creased in thought. "We've got no choice. We've got to take the river. We're trapped. Let's not waste any more time. In we go!"

Without further consideration, both boys stuffed their *yarmulkes*[1] into their pants' pockets and waded into the river, struggling to maintain their balance as the rushing water pounded against them, sweeping them downstream. They soon lost half their gear in the rapids as they tried to grasp protruding rocks and branches while moving through the water. The current was so powerful the boys found it impossible to wade across to the other side, and instead found themselves urged on down-river, deeper and deeper into the 'forbidden territory,' swept helplessly by the current. Several times they lost their grips on rocks or on the hanging branches of nearby trees overlapping the bank. The water was getting deeper as the boys were forced midstream and swept rapidly away, farther and farther into the unknown.

Moshe gasped for air as the wild, zigzagging current rolled him over and over, casting him about like a twig. He had been a good swimmer in school, but here the water wouldn't allow

[1]*yarmulkes*—skullcaps [Yiddish].

him to apply his techniques. Here there were different rules for swimming. Simcha, too, struggled as he was swept onto his back and then swirled around onto his stomach, his face dunked into the cold water. He swallowed a lot of the water and was momentarily thankful that it wasn't salty.

The boys were thrown about in the river for what seemed to be an eternity, their clothes tattered and their arms, legs, and faces cut in many places by the sharp rocks against which they were tossed and scraped. At least they could each still catch sight of the other. Then Moshe noticed a giant log, the remains of a fallen tree, thrashing about several yards from the far side of the river, not much farther downstream. He tried to yell to Simcha about it but each time he opened his mouth, it filled with water.

"Over there!" he finally managed to yell, coughing violently and choking. Simcha struggled as best as he could to get near the log, and as he swept past Moshe, he grabbed him by the remains of his shirttail and dragged him toward the log. The boys grabbed the log and kicked their legs as fast and as hard as they could, propelling themselves closer to the bank of the other side. They made their way, inch by inch, to the shore. Slowly, wearily, and shivering from the dampness and cold, the two crawled up the bank on their hands and knees, panting, and slumped against a tree. Almost as one they glanced up at the branches to make sure there wasn't any boa constrictor waiting around.

They lay ten minutes, out of breath and shivering, when Moshe noticed that a long crocodile on the far bank of the river was eyeing him curiously. "We have some more company, Simcha," he sighed. Simcha was wringing out his *yarmulka*. He looked up at Moshe expectantly.

"I hope this isn't your father's idea. I mean, one thing after another. It's beginning to feel unreal, you know. Like a... uh... a set up."

The crocodile slowly lowered itself into the river and swam underwater. The boys watched the crocodile as it glided surely across the river...toward them. Just as it was about to crawl out of the water, the boys jumped to their feet to run once more. Suddenly, they heard a very loud, earthshaking rumbling from above the stony mountains which flanked the river. Looking up toward the strange sounds, they saw several huge rocks tumble down on their side of the mountain. Immediately they jumped for cover, dashing farther inland and pressing themselves against a huge, aging tree. They watched the heavy stones crash down into the river, some of them crushing the crocodile as it attempted to swim away.

"A miracle!" Moshe exclaimed. "A miracle!"

"So were the ants, Moshe. They scared off the cat. And the snake scared us off so we could see the approaching ants in time."

"Great. Wonderful. Miracles all over the place. But what are we doing here? We're lost. We're far off from that trail, far from the rock. Waikiki is probably trying to call us from atop that cliff we were camped near. He's probably worried sick."

"Not as sick as us! Simcha, do you realize that we've no idea of how to get back there. Every tree looks the same. Every bush. We were able to see the river from atop the rock we climbed yesterday, but we can't seem to see the rock from the river. What a weird world. And you're feeling sorry for Waikiki!"

They sat down again to rest. They were filthy and wet and exhausted. As they recuperated from their most recent challenge they looked around them. It was a magnificent river, dangerous but magnificent. Both banks were bordered by towering walls of rock. The only problem, the boys began to realize, was that the area to which they had been swept by the river was nearly impossible to pass through on land, except in one direction, and that was downstream, farther away from where they had come. To go back toward the campsite would require another swim in the river, this time upstream. They had found it difficult enough swimming with the current; there would be no way they could swim against such a powerful flow. To attempt to retrace their steps on land would require the legs of a fly, for they would have to climb horizontally along the walls of the vertical rock cliffs which towered above them.

They looked at one another helplessly.

"Listen," said Simcha, trying to keep his voice hopeful. "We really have only one choice. We can walk only where the ground is level, even though it's not going to get us back. Eventually, we're bound to find a way back. The mountains may end further downstream, and maybe we can somehow cross the river and detour around…"

"You sound like a safari guide," Moshe interrupted, nervously trying to smooth his wet thick blond hair. "Too many 'ifs' and 'maybes,' and it doesn't console me. I'm exhausted and worried. We've lost our supplies. We have no food, no sleeping bags, and no water. We have no idea where we are or where we're going. I've never been more frightened in my life." Moshe threw his head back and took a deep breath.

"Gee, you don't sound scared," Simcha said, swallowing hard.

Moshe laughed. "I would start screaming if I wasn't so tired and bruised. But you know, even though I'm scared, I'm also excited. I mean, I'm kind of getting comfortable with being afraid. I'm learning that fear is nothing to be afraid of."

Simcha looked at Moshe in surprise. "Boy, this trip sure has made *you* philosophical. What do *you* think we should do?"

"I guess your idea is our only reasonable option. We really have no choice—unless you're in the mood for climbing straight up a wall or wrestling with the river again!"

"No way," said Simcha, shaking his head.

Even though their impulse was to continue resting, they knew that they should keep on going. Though it was still early

morning, the last thing they wanted was to be lost at night.

The boys rose and walked on along the narrow ridge separating the raging river and the rocky cliffs. In different circumstances they might have appreciated the beauty of their surroundings. Tall pink and gray storks stalked the river's edge; other large, colorful birds flew low in search of fish. The sounds of shrieking birds and insects were almost muted by the roar of the river. They walked for several hours in the humid heat, becoming increasingly anxious about not finding any way to detour and turn back. The wall of rock just went on and on, as did the river, winding its way sharply through the canyon. The possibility they would not find a route back became more and more likely. Walking, they realized, did not seem to be the solution. It was probable they would have to turn back and eventually forge the river once more. They reached a small clearing with a clear spring running down the stone wall into the river. They quenched their dry throats and sat down, despondent and famished.

As they sat down to rest, Moshe noticed several clusters of purple berries growing in some of the surrounding brush. He pointed at them and asked Simcha whether he thought they would be safe to eat. "I don't know, Moshe. I don't know how to tell. The only way, I think, is to try just a little piece of one." He reached for a berry and peeled off the soft, juicy skin. After studying the texture of its meat, he licked the berry to see if it tasted sweet. "Tastes like cranberries," Simcha said, making a face as he sucked in his cheeks and concentrated on the taste. "I don't think they're cranberries, though. They also taste like boysenberries." He threw the berry away and tore off a whole of cluster of berries. "They're probably safe, Moshe. If they weren't safe, why would they taste so sweet?"

"Simcha! Do you think you're being logical?"

Simcha shrugged. "How am I supposed to know? I'm just trying to use my instincts!"

"Maybe we shouldn't eat them," cautioned Moshe.

"I really think they're okay, though I could be wrong—I'm a city boy, not a country boy like you. But look at that bird by the river, wasn't it just around here? I bet it was eating these berries. Anyway, I know I'm hungry, and we need to eat one way or another. If anything, we'll probably just get an upset stomach, which is okay with me because then I wouldn't feel so hungry anymore!" With that, Simcha bit into the cluster he was holding in his hand.

Moshe reluctantly joined him. He knew that just because a berry was sweet did not mean it was safe. But he decided to drink lots of water so that maybe any bad effects the berries had would be diluted.

After another hour of sitting and talking, the boys became weary from the hectic adventures of the morning and dozed off in the lazy warm sunlight.

CHAPTER 7

Confronting a Legend

A Mezuzah¹ in the Jungle

Simcha and Moshe walked along merrily, singing Hebrew songs and feeling really good about having been able to scale the seemingly impossible-to-climb stone wall of the mountain. Reaching its top had been so satisfying that they could do nothing but sing and shout with delight, pausing to hear their echoes in neighboring mountains. In the distance—and this had made them even more glad and excited—they could see the tiny outline of Waikiki and the other two guides waving at them from the next mountain top, jumping in celebration.

Simcha stopped Moshe as they approached the edge of the mountain. "Moshe, let me explore a little before you take another step. I don't want you falling off the cliff." He then walked to the cliff's edge to see if he could find a reasonable route down. But he had taken one step too many, and the loose rocks beneath

¹mezuzah—a small roll of parchment on which is handwritten verses from the Bible. It is attached to the right side of the doorpost of Jewish homes, honoring the biblical commandment to inscribe the words of G-d "on the doorposts of thy house and upon thy gates" [Hebrew].

his feet gave way, throwing him off balance. Simcha held his breath as he fell off the mountain and into oblivion.

"Simcha, you okay? Simcha?"

It was the voice of Moshe. Moshe shook Simcha awake. "You okay?"

"Yeah, I'm all right," said Simcha, sitting upright and wiping his perspiring face with the back of his hand. "My head is spinning, though...and my stomach is turning inside out. I had this dream that I was falling off a cliff. But before I fell we found Waikiki and the others."

"Gee, I sure hope those berries were okay," said Moshe worriedly. Simcha's dark brown eyes seemed even more intense in contrast to his pale, perspiring face.

"Well, how does your stomach feel?" Simcha asked Moshe.

"It feels okay, just a little weird. But my head is spinning a little, and I feel slightly dizzy. I'm really worried about those berries."

"Don't worry about them so much, Moshe. It's probably the heat and humidity. I can't believe how hot it is. It could also be that our bodies are just not accustomed to the kind of exercise we've been doing!"

Moshe grinned wearily. "Very funny. I think you ought to drink something anyway to try to wash the berries out of your system."

"Good idea. But I think I also feel kind of funny because of my dream. I really had the feeling I was falling from great heights. Have you ever had a dream where you felt physically as if you were really falling? I mean my heart was speeding when you woke me."

"Yup. It's really amazing how real things like that feel in a dream. Your body acts the same way it would if it were actually happening."

The boys suddenly became silent. Once more they remembered that they were hopelessly lost. No, worse—they were trapped, with only one way to go, deeper into the jungle. They washed up and drank some more from the spring. Then they started out on their journey to uncertainty. They walked on hesitantly, a part of them reluctant to move farther from where they ought to be going, and another impelling them forward in the hope that they would find a way to circumvent the mountains and detour back upstream.

As they walked they noticed the river was becoming narrower and narrower, twisting and turning ever so sharply through the dark, eerie canyon. It was hard to think of the actual time of day because although it was afternoon, little of the sun managed to bend its brilliant rays far enough to reach them. It was becoming increasingly difficult for them to walk along the bank of the river as well, which narrowed along with the river, pinning the boys against the canyon wall. At several points where the river seemed extremely narrow, they thought of trying to cross to the opposite, more spacious shore, but the force of the rapids and the fresh memory of battling for their lives in the water was more than enough to dissuade them.

What little level ground remained to walk on now became rocky and wet, the water of the raging river spraying stones and trees as it swept by. The boys welcomed the spray because the air was thinning in this very narrow region of the canyon, and although the sun hadn't quite been able to penetrate, the narrow stony enclosure was constricted enough to generate its own heat.

Slowly they plodded along the slippery bank, pressing their bodies against the wall of the canyon—which seemed to be closing in on them. They could hardly see the sky now. Looking up they saw only the towering stone wall and its wild brush. The roaring of the rushing river was gradually being replaced by an even noisier roar, the thunder of a waterfall in the distance. They felt both frightened and excited as they approached the booming cataract at the next bend, which poured tons of silt-laden water into the deeper channel from high atop the canyon.

Cautiously, and shivering from the damp chill created by the soaking of the falling water, the boys made their way underneath the heavy downpour, gripping and pressing against the wet, slippery underbelly of the waterfall. They tried shouting to one another as they edged their way between the confining, but dry, space between the falls and the canyon wall, but neither could make out what the other was saying amid the thudding noise of the cascading river.

Reaching safety, they sighed with relief, each hoping they would not have to cross that hurdle again, but realizing that they might indeed have to, unless they could find some other route out. They continued to follow the river, which now seemed to pick up speed and rush even faster and more violently. "Wonder why it's suddenly speeding like that," said Moshe.

"Maybe the ground level is sloping downward more steeply around the next bend," speculated Simcha.

At the bend, they were hard put to discern the far bank. They had to put their feet partially into the river. Holding tightly to jagged rock outcroppings, they carefully navigated this very sharp bend. It was a little wider than the others and took several more minutes to traverse. Simcha, climbing ahead, was the first to see the far side of this wild bend. What he saw surprised him, for there was nothing but emptiness, as the river suddenly, without any warning, dropped hundreds of feet downward into a very large pool which, in turn, branched out into several other rivers, each flowing in a different direction.

The boys energetically gripped the canyon wall as they gazed at the terrifying but breathtaking view. The rush of the falling water was so loud Simcha had to shout. "This sure would make anyone think it was the end of the world," he bellowed.

"Waikiki and the other guides thought they'd already seen it," Moshe shouted back. "They should only see this!"

"Hey!"

"What?!"

"What are you going to do now?"

"How do I know? You're in the lead, Simcha! I've been following *you!*"

"Well, how about you taking over now?! I'm getting tired of calling all the shots!"

"Thanks a lot! Where am I supposed to go?! This is the end of the world!"

"Well, we can't go any further, that's for sure! We'll have to turn back!" shouted Simcha.

"Turn back to where? We'll be trapped forever in this forsaken place!"

Moshe craned his neck and peered over Simcha's trembling shoulders at the stunning scenery hundreds of feet below. Surrounding the shimmering rivers were lush tropical trees, some with pink and purple flowers, others with orange-colored fruits. "Look, Simcha! Look at those trees! Fruit trees! Look at all those colorful fruits down there. The place is crawling with color and food! Maybe... I'll bet there's probably a way to get down there on foot! It looks more manageable! Maybe there's a road or a trail that goes around the mountains!"

"It doesn't look like it from here, Moshe! There's nothing around here but more canyons, most of them even higher than the ones we just came through!"

"But we should try! Look at those fruit trees! A jungle full! Boy am I starving!"

Simcha strained his eyes and craned his neck trying to locate a foot-path. Moshe was right. The jungle below was laden with fruit. Maybe there was even some kind of village down there as well. The trees looked as if they were neatly arranged, growing in rows, almost as if it was somebody's orchard. They looked like...no...yes! They looked like the trees on the ancient coin of Asher the boys had found in the cave in the Galilee. Simcha's heart pounded fiercely. He had placed the coin in his shirt pocket before they had left Nairobi. Had it remained there through all the climbing, swimming and running? He unsnapped his shirt pocket and took a breath of relief when his fingers felt the coin. He had forgotten all about it. He pulled it out and examined the engraving of the tree. It definitely was a fruit tree just like the ones growing below.

Simcha showed the coin to Moshe, pointing out the similarity between the trees. But Moshe was skeptical. "Aw, come on. You don't mean to tell me you think this is the river Sambatyon, and the daughter of Asher lives here with the ten lost tribes, do you?" Moshe said, looking at Simcha with surprise. Simcha always seemed to think everything was connected in some mysterious way. He could drive a person crazy.

Simcha was insistent. "What about the falling rocks? The ones that killed the crocodile?"

"Rocks fall all the time in mountainous regions. Remember when we were travelling to Pirate's Cove, and we saw all those signs warning cars about falling rocks? Come on, Simcha. Don't let this whole thing get to you. Fruit trees like these grow all over the world. The tribe of Asher's got no monopoly on them, you know."

"I know. I guess I'm just looking for some logic in all this mess. Some hope. Anything…, even if it's just a crazy fantasy."

Simcha moved one step back to get closer to where Moshe was standing. He wasn't usually afraid of heights, but this view was dizzying. As he turned around he suddenly lost his footing on the slippery layer of moss which blanketed the stony ground. The dream he had had of falling off a cliff almost became reality. He desperately reached out for something to grab onto. Moshe was out of reach, but a long, leafy, thick vine suspended from above was near enough to grasp, and as he did so, both his feet slipped off the edge and he hung there, swinging, kicking, and screaming.

Moshe, in panic, wrapped his left arm around a protruding tree root and tried to extend his right arm out to Simcha. But

Simcha, kicking, swung too far away for Moshe to reach him. "Stop kicking!" yelled Moshe. "Stop kicking, and you'll stop swinging!"

Simcha did as he was told and hung onto the vine until it came to a halt, nearly smacking him against the stone wall of the canyon. "Moshe! Moshe, look! Look!" Simcha yelled excitedly as he held to the vine over the steep drop. Moshe's eyes followed Simcha's forefinger, which pointed upward. Just around the sharp bend, right above the river's sudden drop, was a cave, several yards up the canyon wall. From where Simcha hung, he could see a lit torch flickering wildly at the mouth of the cave. "Someone lives up there! I see a torch! Let's go! We're saved!"

Simcha climbed clumsily up the stone cliff, using the heavy vine for support as he clambered up the wall like a monkey. Moshe held onto the vine, trying to keep it from moving, while Simcha drew closer to the mysterious cave. When he saw Simcha disappear into the mouth of the canyon wall, Moshe also began to climb, kicking against the surface of the mountain. His legs were still stiff and strained from yesterday's climb, and they ached from bruises he had gotten from rocks in the river. He climbed slowly but steadily. Simcha waited for him at the mouth of the cave and extended his arms toward him. Moshe held onto the vine with one hand while giving Simcha his other hand. With Simcha's help he leaped into the mouth of the cave.

"Doesn't that lit torch attached to the wall of the cave look like a flaming *mezuzah?!*" exclaimed Simcha.

"Oh, come on, Simcha! We're in Africa!" Moshe said. But then, after a minute, he noticed something else, at the other side of the cave's opening, directly opposite the torch. "You're not going to believe this, but there *is* a scroll embedded in the wall of the cave right by the opening. See it?"

Simcha turned his head to look. "It really does look like a *mezuzah*. I wonder what it can be!"

Simcha removed the torch from the wall and walked cautiously through the cavern, curious to see if there were any more signs of life. He spotted what seemed to be the beginning of a spiraling stairwell leading downward.

"Moshe! Come quickly! You're not going to believe what's here!"

Moshe walked through the dark cavern to where Simcha stood with the torch. His mouth dropped open in astonishment. Together they stepped slowly down the rocky stairs, Simcha leading the way with the torch. The boys moved slowly down, deep into the dark belly of the mountain. Deeper and deeper they walked, their hearts racing in nervous excitement as they followed the spiraling stone steps downward. They could feel the air thinning as they descended. Even the fire was starting to go out, struggling for oxygen. The boys were becoming dizzy from the lack of oxygen, and the flame seemed about to extinguish, when the stairwell began to broaden and the boys saw the welcome sight of sun rays piercing the darkness of the cavern. Soon they reached another opening, this one at ground level, overlooking the pool formed by the falling river.

They found a second scroll embedded at the mouth of the cave's ground exit. They were about to examine it when they heard footsteps in the nearby brush. The boys froze, waiting anxiously to see who or what was approaching. Simcha gulped hard. The stories he had heard of cannibals when he was a young child suddenly crossed his mind. To his amazement, two bearded men garbed in flowing robes of many colors approached. They don't look like cannibals, Simcha thought to himself. The men walked up to the boys with friendly smiles on their faces.

"*Shalom!*" exclaimed one, his wide smile revealing bright white teeth. He was a tall burly man with powerful-looking arms. The second man was slimmer but also muscular. He spoke to the boys in a language which resembled Hebrew but seemed somewhat different. The boys, dumbfounded, remained silent, not understanding what the man was trying to say. Clearing his throat, the burly man, who noticed the boys' puzzled expressions, seemingly repeated what his companion had said, but much more slowly. The boys found they could discern his words though they were astonished by what they were hearing.

"Welcome to Sambatyon, friends. We have been expecting you," the man said in Hebrew. It was more of a biblical Hebrew, the boys realized, the style used in the Torah. "You have been through so much. Come with us and we shall lead you to her Royal Highness."

"Royal Highness?" Moshe blurted in Hebrew. "You mean, like a queen?"

"No, friend, not 'like' a queen. She *is* a queen. Her name is Serach, and she is the revered daughter of our father Asher. My name is Michael, of the tribe of Asher. And my friend here is Vafsi, of the tribe of Naftali—the fastest man alive."

Vafsi smiled. "He always says that. I can run fast, true, but I have not yet raced every man, so I do not consider myself the fastest."

"Modesty, modesty," chided Michael, patting his friend on the back. "Come on, you two, follow us. We'll get you cleaned up and fed and then you will meet our queen, bless her."

The stunned boys followed the men through the orchard and into the jungle along a cobble-stoned path. After a few minutes they arrived at a clearing surrounded by two of the branches of the river. Speckled across the clearing and atop several small, wooded hills, were hundreds of homes, each very distinct and artistically designed. The boys marvelled at what they saw and were having difficulty overcoming the first shock of finding themselves amid their long-lost kinsmen.

Serach

"Is this for real?" whispered Simcha to Moshe as they walked. "Can we really be in Sambatyon? It seems as though we have stepped into the pages of the *midrash* about the ten lost tribes. Are we dreaming?"

"It sure is a great dream if that's what it is! But dream or no dream, I'm starving! Maybe they'll give us some food!" said Moshe, licking his lips at the thought of food. After a moment, he added in a worried voice, "Maybe it was the berries we ate. They may have done something crazy to us. I mean, maybe they were like some kind of drug."

"You don't suppose we are hallucinating all this, do you?"

"I don't know what to make of it," Moshe said, shaking his head in wonder at all the day's events. Simcha turned to him with a questioning face.

Moshe smiled awkwardly. "Just promise me, Simcha, that whatever happens, you won't leave me here."

"Leave you? What are you saying? Why would I leave you? Are you feeling alright?" Simcha asked gently. Moshe's eyes were filled with tears.

"I don't know why I said that. My head's feeling awfully funny. And I have this strange scary feeling that you're fading in and out. Your voice keeps fading in and out." Moshe bit his bottom lip. "I sure miss my father. Boy is he going to kill me—that is *if* we survive!"

Simcha felt frightened as well, but he tried not to let it get to him. These men seemed nice enough. Maybe they could help them get back to Nairobi. Whatever was going on didn't seem dangerous—just very weird.

"Moshe?"

"Yes?"

"Don't worry so much. I think we are better off now then we were lost in the jungle. And you know I'll never leave you— don't you?"

"Yes. I'm sorry. I'm okay now. I was just a little scared."

The two men had been walking ahead of them. Now they waited for the boys in front of one of the houses. When the boys caught up with the men Michael bid Vafsi good-bye and ushered the boys into his house. The interior of the structure made the boys even dizzier than they already were. The house was sparsely furnished and had spiraling stone staircases leading to various lofts. Moshe couldn't tell whether the house was ancient or space-age since it seemed to be designed with both in mind. To Simcha, the beautiful stone interior reminded him of a museum exhibition, with a combination of modern and ancient art.

Michael disappeared into what appeared to be a small cave situated at the rear of the house, and then quickly reappeared with an elegantly designed clay jug and three cups. He poured the boys a cold drink from the jug and placed the cups on a table nearby. The boys sat down at the table and waited for their host to join them, since he had also poured a cup for himself. As he moved about the house preparing something for the boys to eat, Michael noticed that they were waiting.

"I see you're not as thirsty as I had assumed," he said in Hebrew, cutting up some fruit.

"Oh, we're just waiting for you," Moshe explained, speaking slowly, trying not to use too many modern Hebrew words.

"For me?" said Michael, his eyebrows raised all the way. "For me? You are thirsty, and you are waiting for me? But why?"

"That's our custom. Where we come from we wait for the host to begin eating or drinking before the guests do."

"Is that so? Is that your custom? I see, I see." Michael chuckled to himself. "It's not a Jewish custom, is it? Pray tell it's not."

The perplexed boys looked at one another. "I don't know what kind of custom it is exactly," Simcha replied. "It's just the way we were raised, I guess."

"Interesting. Very interesting," muttered Michael as he slit a melon. "Wait for the host to start eating. Very strange, but interesting."

Michael placed a wooden tray laden with a colorful assortment of delicious fruits on the table before the boys. Their mouths watered at the sight of food, but noticing that Michael sat down with a plate, they restrained themselves from eating, waiting for him to make the first move. He didn't. He just sat there, watching the boys observe him.

"My dear friends. Let me explain our custom in Sambatyon, a custom of etiquette taught to us by our ancestors. I think this custom goes back for more than two or three thousand years. We, too, are Israelites. We are what you know as 'the lost tribes.' As far as we are concerned, however, we're not lost. We just do not wish to be found."

The boys were losing their patience, hoping their host would take his first bite, or drink, or, at the very least, permit them to start without him. "So you're very hungry and thirsty, I see," he said, smiling at them. "It is very clear to me that you would like nothing more than to fill your stomachs with these delicious mangoes, peaches, and melons. But I want to teach you something. You see, you two are strangers, guests at my table. I am fulfilling the deed of hospitality, a very important deed, what you people call 'a big *mitzvah*[2].' Now tell me, does your custom of waiting for the host to start make any sense? Am I fulfilling any *mitzvah* by inviting you into my home and then allowing you to starve while I'm busy running about doing my business or just talking? Sounds unreasonable, no? Our custom is very simple. When you invite someone into your home and place food on the table, this in itself is a clear gesture that you want the guest to eat, that you permit the guest to eat, and the guest does not have to wait for the host to join him. Understand?"

The boys were surprised. Michael, of course, was right. Didn't Abraham allow his three guests to eat first? And wasn't he a model of hospitality?

"You're right, Michael. We must be following European custom," acknowledged Simcha. "May we?" he said, reaching for

²*mitzvah*—good deed [Hebrew].

a peach. Michael nodded. Moshe also grabbed a peach and together the boys said a blessing before taking a big bite. Michael chuckled as the boys feasted on the juicy peaches and melon slices. As Michael's chuckle turned into roaring laughter it was suddenly interrupted by the appearance of a tall, beautiful woman with big round green eyes. She smiled warmly at the boys and approached the table with a tray full of what looked like pita bread.

"Friends," Michael announced, "this is the most special person in my entire world. She is the bone of my bone, flesh of my flesh. She is Tamar, my wife."

"I heard you two were coming, so I prepared some bread. But be careful. It's freshly baked and steaming hot."

"How long have you all known we were coming?" asked Simcha, trying to keep the surprise he felt from showing in his voice.

"From the moment she told us. Yesterday some time," replied Tamar, matter-of-factly.

"She?" inquired Moshe, and then he attempted a guess. "You mean Serach?"

"Yes. Michael already told you about her?"

"Well, Simcha told me about her a while ago. He had learned about Serach and the ten lost tribes in a *midrash*."

"A *what*?"

"A *midrash*," explained Simcha, "is a collection of the teachings of the rabbis from about fifteen hundred to two thousand years ago, teachings about everything…philosophy, commentary on the Torah, stories like the legend of Sambatyon—which, it appears, is no legend at all." Simcha concluded with a chuckle.

"We have similar collected studies," said Tamar. "We study these teachings in groups, but without books. Face to face, parents to children, teachers to students. According to the dates you have given, our ancestors were driven from the holy soil about five hundred years before your *midrash* was developed, so we are not familiar with it. Although *she* might be. She knows everything, you know. You will meet her soon. And, by the way, do not use that term—ten lost tribes—when you speak to her. We are not lost, no more so than the tribes you two belong to. We are very happy and satisfied here. One day we shall return to the holy soil, but for now this soil is our home. And we do not wish to be found."

"What about *us*?" asked Moshe, a little nervously. "*We* found you. Will you let us go? Will you show us how to get back to my father? Or at least Waikiki? He's our guide. We promise not to tell anyone where you are. You can even blindfold us."

"Certainly you will be allowed to return," laughed Tamar. "We are not your captors, nor are you the first to have become lost and ventured into our province. Others have, too, though not many. They were all certainly allowed to return. We do not fear that we will be found because no one can come here intentionally. Those who wandered in here did exactly that, wandered. They were lost. The falling rocks which guard the entrance to Sambatyon do not fall upon those who wander here because they are lost, only upon those who seek to disturb our peace."

"You mean you're not worried that these wandering people will then inform others of your whereabouts?" asked Simcha.

"No. If they get in here it is because they are lost. If they are lost they cannot figure out how to return. If they attempt to deliberately seek us out, the river Sambatyon will stop them."

"How do you get lost people like us out of here? I hope it's not by the same way we came," asked Moshe hopefully.

"Oh no! Do not worry about that. We have a secret passage out of Sambatyon. Those who are led out are first temporarily blinded so they will be unable to rediscover the passage. We send an escort to guide them to the other side, and then, after a brief time, their vision is restored on its own. The blindness is caused by an herbal extract."

"Wow," the boys muttered as they resumed their eating.

Michael brought them some water to wash their hands with before they said a blessing over the bread. Soon after, they washed again in preparation for their meeting with Serach. As they walked through the village of Sambatyon, small children, also dressed in colorful robes, waved at them, smiling excitedly as they walked by. They felt like heroes being paraded through a city. Some of the people, they noticed, were darker than others, but all, it seemed, were quite tall, thin and muscular. Michael and Tamar answered the boys' questions as they walked, explaining how the region of Sambatyon was under the dominion of Serach, the ruler of that part of the jungle.

"Now you understand why that leopard ran back up the hill," explained Michael, after the boys had told him of their adventures. "No doubt it was the power of our blessed queen, for she watched over you from the time you entered the forbidden zone. She is a prophetess."

"No, Michael," a voice suddenly said. It was a soft, gentle, and compassionate voice, and it came from behind them. They turned around to face a tall, very handsome woman with piercing blue eyes that seemed to look directly through them. Tamar and Michael bowed low and introduced the startled boys to Serach, the daughter of Asher the son of Jacob. The boys stared, mouths agape. They had expected to meet a three-thousand-year-old wrinkled bag of bones, and instead found themselves facing a tall, strong-looking woman whose age they could not really tell. Her eyes were wild and beautiful, yet exuded a calmness that put the boys immediately at ease. You wouldn't have thought she was three thousand years old. Thirty, maybe.

"I am Serach. But I do not perform miracles. Only G-d does. The Creator of nature is the only One who can alter nature. But, out of the kindness we have all yet to earn, G-d has granted some of us the honor of serving as instruments for the performance of miracles in the physical world, miracles which therefore seem more obvious than the indirect, concealed miracles which

G-d alone performs every moment...the miracle of our bodies functioning, of wind blowing, or of an unattended infant eluding a source of deadly danger. If I had not had a hand in it, the leopard would have been distracted in some other fashion, perhaps in some less direct way." Serach spoke beautifully. Her Hebrew, Simcha realized, was the pure Hebrew of the Bible.

"But what about the ants?" asked Simcha.

"The leopard had more time than he needed to prey upon one of you before the ants approached. You must have realized this. I attempted to redirect the ants from you but I can only perform so-called miracles as G-d wills them. In this case I was powerless. Destiny forced you in this direction." Serach paused and looked at Moshe. "You needed to be informed of something which I will tell you about later. And so you were led here by the ants, by the river, and by the narrow canyon path. There is a reason, you see, for everything. Even, and perhaps especially, when something seems meaningless, purposeless. Life is cleverly disguised by experiences which test our faith and our awareness of G-d and of our responsibilities to ourselves and to others. And tests serve to strengthen us."

"I often dreamed of this," said Simcha, "since I first learned the story of Sambatyon and the ten los...uh...and the ten tribes. I remember thinking about how I wanted to meet you, the daughter of Asher, and how I'd have millions of questions to ask you and things I'd want to discuss with you. And here I am, a dream come true, and I don't know what to say."

Serach smiled and sat down on a rock while gesturing for everyone else to sit down as well. As she spoke to the boys, men, women, and children slowly gathered around them trying to catch every word. Simcha and Moshe felt they were in paradise. They couldn't quite believe where they were and with whom they were speaking. It was all too good to be true. The feeling was one of sweetness, of total peace, as they sat listening to the words of this remarkable woman.

"It is far easier to yearn for something than to actually have it," she said. "Many times we feel this urgent desire for something, and then when we finally attain it we realize that the feeling of wanting it was much stronger than the feeling we now have after getting it. Or there are other experiences, such as that of observing a beautiful sunset, which is enjoyable only if you observe from a distance. If you were so overwhelmed by the beautiful horizon that you jumped into a boat and rowed toward it, it would vanish. It can't be reached. And all of this is because of your soul. The spiritual energy within you. The real *you* deep inside. The driver of your body, your mind, and your emotions. The soul, you see, desires much more than the body and its faculties are capable of providing. It yearns for more than the physical world can accommodate. That is why people have a hard time being satisfied with what they have. If you have a hundred coins you are likely to desire two hundred, and if you have obtained that, three hundred. Not because you need more money all the time, but simply because you are confusing your feelings. Your soul desires more spiritual exposure, such as studying Torah, prayer, helping others; but your body often mistranslates this spiritual need. So it is all right that you do not know what to say now that you are here. Your desire to speak was your mind's translation of the boundless yearning of your soul, the yearning, perhaps, to reconnect to your past. So now you are here. You need say nothing at all."

"I understand now," said Simcha. He then smiled and bashfully asked Serach, "Would it be asking too much if you taught us a few things we could take with us?"

Serach laughed softly. After a thoughtful pause, she spoke. "Always be children," she said. Everyone around her nodded in agreement. "Do not ever stop, not even for one moment, feeling like a child. We are, after all, called 'children of Israel,' for our father Jacob—Israel—never ceased to see us as children even after we had grown far into adulthood. When he mourned

the loss of Joseph, he would often tell us that even if Joseph was alive and was found he would still mourn over the loss of his childhood. When we go through hard times we forget so easily how to be children, how to look at the world with simplicity, as a child does; how to see things for what they are, not for what they seem; how to expect so very little and appreciate so very much. We forget how to marvel over the sight of a butterfly, even an ant, and to love life just for that moment alone. Always be children, even when you reach a hundred. That way you will be able to enjoy more of life, for you will be much more aware of life both outside of you and inside of you—your feelings, your thoughts.

"Also, do not be afraid of fear. Fear is the feeling G-d gave you to protect you from dangerous things, to make you more alert. It is just an alarm that is set to go off for your defense—nature's way of protecting your life. But do not allow it to take control of you, and do not become obsessed with it. The same goes for any of the other feelings human beings are endowed with—love, hate, jealousy, greed, honor, pride. They all have their place, their time for expression, and their purpose. The infant is not even afraid of fire, but is curious about it, innocently excited by the dancing flames. We are not fearful creatures by nature. We *learn* fear. Most of our fears we learn from the fears our parents or our friends may have, or from frightening experiences that linger in our minds because we fail to turn off the alarm even after the danger has passed. So, do not be afraid even when you are alone and in the darkness. You would not be afraid if your parents were with you, so do not be afraid when you are alone, either, for you are *never* all alone. G-d is with you everywhere, every moment.

"Respect all creatures. Honor all people, for every man is just as much the work of the Creator as were Adam and Eve. Remember that your ancestor Abraham, though in pain after his circumcision at an advanced age, ran as fast as his feet could carry him to welcome what he assumed were three pagan wayfarers. He did not ask them what religion they practiced or what race they belonged to or which synagogue they attended or which rabbi they believed in. He did not judge them by their appearance, nor did he see them as anything but fellow human beings, and he treated them accordingly. Thus we must certainly not judge one another as Jews, nor show less respect for Jews different than us, less knowledgeable or less observant of Torah. We must honor all Jews as our brothers and sisters, and respect their views when they differ from ours. We may share what we know with others, but never alienate them on account of any differences.

"Remember that although we were forged into a single nation in the kiln of Egyptian bondage, G-d nevertheless chose to preserve our distinct tribal identities. During the desert journey Israel was divided into its tribal components. In the land of Israel itself, our people were again divided according to tribe to teach us the importance of recognizing that no two people are alike. The breastplate which hung over the *kohen's*[3] chest during the era of the Holy Temple had twelve stones upon it, each representing a different tribe, each a very different color. True unity between people can come about only through *mutual respect* of each other's differences. If two groups will not respect one another's differing views, then I can almost guarantee you that each of those groups will eventually experience conflict within themselves, too. As you must have noticed, we all wear clothing of many colors. Our father Jacob made a garment of many colors for Joseph to wear, and we have adopted this as our garb as constant reminder that this is exactly what we are as a people—a single garment of many colors. A rainbow has many colors, but they all originate from one simple, colorless light."

A young man approached Serach and whispered something to her. She nodded and turned back to the boys. "Would you

[3]*kohen*—priest [Hebrew].

like to join us as we recite our prayers?"

"You mean, you have prayer books like we do?" asked Simcha. "And synagogues?"

"Well, not exactly. We express our awareness of G-d as the Source of everything we enjoy. We recite from the psalms of King David, for they are worded beautifully and express our feelings with exactness. But we also pray in our own words, each person thanking G-d in his and her own way. In this manner, we come before G-d with both our strengths and our weaknesses, the strength of the perfectly worded psalms, the muscles of our heritage, and the weakness of our own frail, feebly-constructed prayers."

"Why don't you just stick to the perfect expressions of the psalms?" asked Moshe.

"Because I believe G-d seeks not perfection of us, but effort. Also, prayer is not for G-d. It is for humanity. People need to exercise their awareness of G-d in a physical, down-to-earth way, since we are physical beings living in a physical world. Do you not understand? If I pray only in the words of King David, then only a part of me has prayed. The part that represents perfection, the use of the right words, doing all the right things, and so forth. But perfection is not really the sum total of who and what I am. As a human being, I also make mistakes, I forget things. I do not always speak correctly or clearly, maybe even possess habits which are not good. G-d created me with strengths and weaknesses, and so I come before my Creator with both."

"This has always bothered me," said Moshe. "Why did G-d not make us perfect? Why *do* we make mistakes?"

"Actually, my child, the imperfection you see, in the world and in yourself, makes perfection possible. An infant may rise and fall, rise and fall in its attempt to walk. But it is precisely that experience of trial and error that enables the infant ultimately to walk."

"But still—couldn't G-d have created us ready-made in such

a way that we wouldn't have to go through all that trial and error in order to learn things?" Simcha asked.

"Certainly. But why stop there? Why do you think G-d did not create us in such a way that we would not need to eat or drink? Why experience hunger and thirst? And why be capable of experiencing joy? Why not just create us automatically happy?"

"I guess," said Simcha, straining to understand, "that if we had been created already happy we would never know what happiness really is."

"You have answered your own question, Simcha. You see, this is a world of preparation. Here we experience joy, pain; right, wrong; hot, cold; male, female. Here we experience opposite feelings and phenomena in order to appreciate the oneness of G-d and the unimaginable peace that such an awareness brings. But enough talk. We relate to G-d not only through study and prayer, but also through action, by interacting with G-d's creations: nature, people, our feelings. Come, then, and let us celebrate the gifts of life, the samples of G-d's goodness to us, the gift of music."

"I thought we were going to pray now," said Moshe, with a puzzled look on his face.

"We are going to pray," Serach explained, smiling. "But first we will create the proper feelings within ourselves from which our prayers will then emerge. Feelings of joy. Do you want to come before G-d with words that are different than your feelings? Why do you suppose musical instruments and choral singing were always a part of the service when the Holy Temple stood?"

"In our community," Simcha interjected, "we have learned to minimize musical enjoyment in order to remember the destruction of the Temple."

"Aha, I understand," said Serach, rising. She started walking toward the place where the service was to be held, and the boys followed. "And I respect your ways," she continued, "as all Jews must respect the sometimes different ways and customs of different Jewish communities. We, however, feel that, as King Solomon wrote, there is a time to laugh and a time to weep. A mourner may not weep forever. Life must go on. We, too, mourn the loss of the Holy Temple and yearn daily for its return, speedily in our days. But in the meantime, we must not abuse G-d's other life gifts in this world, especially when at times they seem few and far between. Nor must we neglect the opportunities of spiritual growth which they provide. Sometimes, if I were to allow myself to become too sad, I could end up destroying yet another Temple, the Temple that is my body."

The boys followed Serach to a huge circle of men, women, teens, and children, who were waiting for her to join them. When they saw their queen, all rose in respect. Several women began to beat gently on bongo-like instruments, others on cymbals, while a group of men started to play a crude string instrument. At first, the sounds seemed non-melodious to the boys, but soon everyone commenced a low chant that gradually merged in harmony with the instrumentals, soaring higher and higher into the sweetest sound they had ever heard. Simcha's eyebrows shot up in surprise when he suddenly recognized the chant as that of the traditional melody chanted on the High Holy Days. Was it as ancient as Serach, or at least as old as the days of the First Temple, before the tribes were lost? Even Moshe recognized the chant as it grew louder and more pronounced. No wonder, Simcha thought, that the chant was so universal, sung on Rosh Hashanah and Yom Kippur by Jews of all backgrounds, everywhere.

The pace of the chant suddenly quickened, and all were on their feet in celebrative dance. The men and women danced separately, gradually moving apart and forming different circles. The singing and dancing continued for about fifteen minutes, and then there was a heavy, awesome hush as everyone remained still in meditative prayer. The boys were amazed and somewhat uncomfortable about it all since they were unfamiliar with this kind of prayer. A black boy who seemed to be their age appeared from behind them and whispered to them.

"Shalom," he said. "My name is Dan. Would you like to do what we are doing now?"

"Sure," said Simcha, relieved that someone had come over to help them out.

"Good. Then shut your eyes. Not tightly. Be relaxed. Sit down and allow your body to just be at ease. Let your head droop. Just spend a little time simply being, not doing. Allow your lungs to breathe on their own; don't control them. Now, in the quiet and the peace of your mind, become aware of your existence. Just you alone. And gradually become aware of G-d. Now it is just you and G-d, for as our teachers have taught, the worth of the creation of the entire universe is in one person alone. After you have attained this awareness, keep with it until we commence the recitation of psalms."

When the meditative prayers were completed, the people began chanting from the Book of Psalms in harmonious melody and with the accompaniment of instruments. Even small children, the boys noticed, had gotten caught up in the joy and the dance and were now engaged in prayer together with their parrents. It was a truly moving, overwhelmingly beautiful sight to them.

CHAPTER 8

The Holiest of Holies

That night the boys were unable to sleep. For nearly an hour they lay in the special tent that had been set up for them and could do nothing but talk about where they were and with whom. Eventually, they couldn't suppress their curiosity.

Quietly, they dressed and stepped softly into the night. The roadway leading through the community was well lit by fiery torches in front of each hut, casting eerie shadows as they walked. Now that the community was asleep the boys could hear the not too distant roar of the Sambatyon River. Its sounds frightened them as they walked through the strange village, but they were determined to discover what they could about this mysterious place. After all, they were detectives, weren't they? Maybe there were secrets the people of Sambatyon weren't going to reveal to them, things they weren't going to show them.

They came to the opening of a cave, whose passageway was flanked by two flaming torches and stone-sculpted lions with fierce-looking faces.

"Should we look inside?" Moshe asked as they stood outside trying to peer in.

"I don't know, Simcha. Looks foreboding."

"And forbidden."

"But then again, why would it be so open and unattended, and so lit up if you weren't allowed to go in?"

Cautiously, they entered the cave and walked along the well-lit trail which brought them deeper and deeper inside, winding to the left and then to the right and then to the left again, like a snake. As they walked they kept glancing over their shoulders, growing more and more frightened.

Suddenly, a powerful gust swept through the cave, extinguishing all the torches. The boys instantly grabbed each other, freezing in terror as the pitch dark enveloped them. It was now so dark they could almost feel it—if that were possible. They were about to turn back and retrace their steps by feeling along the walls when Simcha noticed something farther along the trail.

"Look, Moshe!" he exclaimed.

Moshe tried looking but it was so dark he couldn't tell where Simcha was pointing. He turned his head about until his eyes caught what Simcha's had: a tiny glow. It was barely visible, and so small that at first it seemed like a spot of flickering light you see sometimes when you shut your eyes. But this light was different. It was definitely not inside their eyelids. Clutching each other, the boys moved toward it.

Strangely, the closer they got to the light, the farther away it glowed, until they walked about fifty feet more, when the glow stopped moving away. As they drew nearer to it, they noticed a second source of light beyond it. And as they got closer to this second light, the original glow disappeared completely. The second light came from around a bend in the trail. The boys followed the light cautiously, trembling. Slowly, they turned the corner. They were suddenly forced to shield their eyes with their arms as they reached the source of light.

"What is it?" Moshe asked, squinting intensely. It seemed as though shielding his eyes with his arm was barely enough, and that the light was penetrating straight through him, blinding him.

"I don't know," replied Simcha, gasping in discomfort as he tried in vain to protect his eyes. "Let's get out of here!"

The boys were about to turn around when the light started to dim rapidly. They hesitated a few moments. Then they walked forward, toward the source of the light: It was an ancient Torah scroll, mounted on a gold-plated structure made of crude stone. The scroll was partially unrolled, draped across the huge stone, and giving off its own light. Their mouths agape, the boys drew themselves closer to the old scroll. They pored over it to discover what made this Torah so different from the ones they had seen in their own synagogues.

"Look at that!" Simcha exclaimed, staring at the sharply illustrated words made of letters with unique, beautifully designed crowns. "The letters are moving! This Torah doesn't read like the ones in *shul*[1]. Look how the letters shift back and forth, forming all different combinations of words."

"Wow!" whispered Moshe. "And all in the same sentences, too. Or lines. I mean, there don't seem to be sentences. It's hard to tell anything because all the letters are right next to each other without any gaps. What kind of Torah is it?"

"Beats me, Moshe. This is really strange. Too bad this cave doesn't have a tour guide."

"Excuse me," came a deep husky voice.

The boys jumped, and quaked as they turned around to look up at a giant of a man. He was very dark and muscular and must have been nearly seven feet tall. He scratched his long curly black beard...and smiled at them.

"Ah. You boys must be our visitors, eh? Don't be frightened. I am Zimri, warrior of Sambatyon. Head of its army."

[1]*shul*—synagogue [Yiddish].

"We didn't know you had an army," said Moshe.

"Rarely are we threatened from the outside, but every now and then we are intruded upon by wicked bands of people who stumble upon us. We are well prepared with a handful of warriors like me. That's all we really need. Ten of us can drive out hundreds of intruders. But I am not here to discuss our army; I am here to discuss your presence in the sacred cave! Probably, no one told you that you are not allowed to enter this area. But now you must leave. Please follow me."

The boys threw a quick, final glance at the strange Torah scroll and walked behind the warrior. As they followed him they studied his impressive, flowing robe, with its silver embroidery of rows of lions. The lions formed a design similar to the familiar Star of David.

"Aren't you going to explain what we just saw?" asked Simcha. "Or are you forbidden to tell us?"

"I was waiting for you to ask," the man said, as they walked through the winding cave. He was rekindling the extinguished torches as they walked. "That Torah is from the time of Moses. It is *the* original scroll and will be kept here until the time of the *Mashiach*[2]."

"Wow!" exclaimed ever skeptical Moshe. "I don't believe it! How come the words move?! How come there are no word cut-offs, or gaps between sentences and paragraphs?"

"Because the Torah is G-d's word. And the word of G-d—like G-d Himself—is infinite, addressing human experience as that experience changes. The word of G-d never changes—just as G-d does not change—but its meaning, how it speaks to us humans, shifts as human experience shifts. In other words, after the *Mashiach* comes, we will read the words of the Torah somewhat differently from the way we read those same words now. The world situation will have changed."

"Awesome! How mysterious. How inspiring!" said Simcha.

[2]*Mashiach*—Messiah [Hebrew].

"As nice as this sounds to you," the warrior Zimri said, "I'm afraid you won't remember it when you leave Sambatyon. There are certain experiences here which are secret, which no one in the outside world can know. That is why none of us can leave Sambatyon. We are the keepers of the secrets, and, in turn, the secrets are our keepers."

Zimri led the boys out of the cave and back to their tent, gently admonishing them to remain there for the rest of the night. The boys complied and, surprisingly enough, were now able to fall asleep, exhausted from the cave expedition.

CHAPTER 9

Warning

*T*he following morning the boys eagerly joined the community in prayer once more and then visited Serach with Michael and Tamar. This time they planned to ask Serach about her miraculous longevity.

Serach laughed heartily. "It's been 3,000 years since anyone has asked me about my age," she said. "Since I am part of the tradition of this community, my age is pretty much taken for granted here, isn't it?" She turned to the two Sambatyon natives, who nodded, then back to the boys. "Yes, it is so: I am the daughter of Asher, son of Jacob, and it is due to a remark made in passing by my grandfather Jacob that I live on and on. Even a statement made in passing by a spiritual giant like Jacob is by no means an ordinary slip-of-the-tongue. It is almost as if G-d has instructed nature to obey the commands of those close to Him."

She continued after a pause. "And so, when I heard my Uncle Joseph was alive in Egypt, I—then a little younger—ran excitedly to tell my grandfather the wonderful news. I had seen him so sad, mourning so long over Joseph's absence, that I could not wait to tell him, but he could not believe the news that his son was still alive. He said to me: 'Ha! Uncle Joseph is still alive like you're going to live forever!' Well, you know the rest. Joseph was indeed alive, and so I live forever."

When Serach had finished speaking, she shut her eyes in deep concentration for a moment, then opened them again and looked at Moshe. "The reason destiny has forced you in this direction, Moshe, is that your father is in serious danger."

Moshe gasped involuntarily. Simcha grasped his arm. Michael and Tamar averted their eyes.

Serach nodded sympathetically at him. "Your father is a very brave man, but unless you reach him by tomorrow evening, he will walk straight into an ambush when he leads our brothers and sisters out of Ethiopia. There is a traitor involved. It is his leading guide. A frightened little man, a soldier. He sides with the Palestinian terrorists. He has deceived your father and will lead him into this ambush. The two of you must leave at once."

Moshe bit his bottom lip. In a small voice he asked, "Will we be able to save him?"

Serach looked at Moshe, her blue eyes giving no clue. "I hope so. You must be quick and use your minds well."

"Where do we go and how can we save him?" asked Moshe urgently.

"You'll know everything you need to know in the proper time."

Before Moshe was composed enough to ask more questions, Tamar withdrew from her pocket a tiny leather pouch. She instructed the boys to tilt their heads back so she could put the drops of the herbal extract into their eyes.

"Uh oh," said Simcha. "Is this when you blind us temporarily?"

"Yes, it is," said Michael. "The extract just feels like drops of water. It's alright. We will carry you on a chair. You will be very comfortable throughout the journey."

The boys looked around one last time, then shrugged at one another. They complied with Tamar's instruction, and she gently put tiny drops of the extract into their eyes. The boys each blinked once, and then saw nothing. They were distressed by the loss of their sight and uncomfortable with their loss of control. As they were being led to a chair suspended by two long poles, Simcha remembered something. He reached deep into his shirt pocket and withdrew the ancient coin they had found in the Galilee.

"I have something for the queen...uh...for Serach," Simcha said to Michael as he was helped up onto the chair carrier.

"She is right here, my friend," said Michael.

Serach took the coin from Simcha. "It is beautiful!" he heard her say. She sounded as if she were sniffling, perhaps crying. "This is the currency of ancient times, from my tribe. Did you find it in the north toward the west?"

"Yes," replied Simcha, wishing he could see the expression on Serach's face. "We were hiking up in the north when we found it. We came upon this pelican, you see, in this cave, and it was wounded and..."

"A pelican?" Serach interrupted. "My, how G-d works in wondrous ways!"

"I don't understand. What do you mean?"

"You will soon understand. Go, now. *Tzetchem l'shalom.*[1] You will know everything you need to know in its proper time. But remember, brothers, the time you spent with us is to be a secret. Your experience here, everything you saw—your meeting me and the others—it is all a secret you must pledge to keep. It is the secret of Sambatyon."

---

[1] *Tzetchem l'shalom*—Go in peace [Hebrew].

CHAPTER 10

A Miracle on the Road

Moshe awoke and tried opening his eyes. They felt exceptionally heavy this morning. "Sambatyon?!" Moshe shouted as he managed to sit up and open his eyes. He found himself sitting in the middle of the jungle.

"You okay?" muttered Simcha, still half asleep.

"Groggy. I'm really groggy. Where are we? I don't even remember going to sleep, do you?"

"No. But boy does my head feel heavy. I don't even remember dreaming, let alone sleeping," said Simcha, sitting up and rubbing his eyes.

"Were you in Sambatyon with me? Did we actually meet Serach?" asked Moshe, a little hesitantly.

Simcha cocked his head toward Moshe. "Yes, I mean, I think so."

"I thought maybe it was all a dream," Moshe said, shrugging.

"Come on, Moshe, it was too real to have been a dream."

Moshe nodded and then suddenly went pale. "Well, if it was all real, then we'd better hurry before something happens to my father!" he cried.

The boys struggled to their feet. They searched around them for some clues as to which direction to take.

"Gee," said Simcha, "I wish Serach had given us some directions."

"She did say that we would know what we needed to know when we needed to know what we needed to know," said Moshe.

"Well, I have no idea..."

Simcha was interrupted just then by some rustling in the nearby brush. He focused his eyes and gasped at what he saw. "There's that bird again! I don't believe it!"

The boys remained still for a long time, trying to digest the experience of rediscovering the wounded pelican nearly a thousand miles from where they had first seen it. It was all so astonishing. Was this the sign that Serach had hinted about when they had mentioned the Galilean pelican?

Together, the boys moved slowly toward the bird, each hoping the mysterious creature would be their ticket out of the thicket. As they drew closer to the bird, it turned away from them and began to wobble through the tall grass. They walked behind it, eager, curious, hopeful, and anxious. Would the bird lead them out, or was it a false clue that would lead them deeper into the jungle?

The pelican continued to wobble through the grass and then started into a thick mass of trees and tall plants whose leaves protruded straight out like green spears. "Ouch!" cried Moshe as one of the long pointed leaves tore at his leg.

"Shhh!" Simcha scolded. "You'll frighten away the bird!" But it was too late. The pelican took to flight.

"Look!" Moshe shouted. "He's not hurt anymore! Look at him fly!"

"That's terrific!" said Simcha in a sarcastic tone of voice. "I'm happy for him. Now, what about us?"

"Let's follow him."

"Follow? We can't fly!"

Without further discussion the boys began to run while trying to watch where the bird was going. As they approached a clearing in the jungle the bird suddenly picked up speed and soared high over a mountain, out of the boys' sight. Frantic, they ran toward the mountain but, to their dismay and frustration, the bird was nowhere to be found.

Simcha sat down on a stone to catch his breath while Moshe paced back and forth in front of him, panting. "You're making me dizzy, Moshe," he said. "Can't you pace somewhere else?"

Moshe stopped in his tracks, his eyes fixed on the opposite end of the clearing, his mouth agape. "I sure can," he replied. "I'll pace on to that road over there!"

Simcha turned around and then quickly jumped to his feet. A paved road sliced through the grassy clearing, winding around the side of the mountain over which the pelican had disappeared. The two ran toward the road as fast as their feet would carry them. Coming around the bend at that very moment was a colorfully decorated late-model van. They ran screaming and waved their arms excitedly, hoping to draw the attention of the van's occupants.

To their joy and relief the van screeched to a halt at the side of the road, sand and dry leaves swirling all around it. The boys ran to the van and approached the driver, a husky red-bearded man with beads of sweat dripping on his forehead. He stared wide-eyed at them, as did his female companion.

"Hi! Can you please help us?" Simcha cried in English. "We're lost. We need to get back to Nairobi, or any place with a telephone."

The couple continued staring blankly at the boys as if in shock. Without shifting his gaze, the man swallowed hard and spoke softly. "Sweets," he said, swallowing again, "do you see what I'm seeing? Or is it just me who's hallucinating?"

"No, Larry," she replied just as softly. "I see them, too."

"*Them?* You mean they're real, then? But what about their heads? Do you see what I see on their heads?"

"Yes, Larry. *Yarmulkes.*"

"Oh no. That means we're both hallucinating. I'm telling you, man, this Kenya heat is a real tripper. Two American Jewish kids with *yarmulkes* wandering around Africa, man. Too much."

Simcha chuckled and introduced himself and Moshe Tamari.

Larry swallowed. Gloria nervously stuffed several pieces of gum into her mouth. Both continued staring at the boys, barely blinking.

"Gloria, sweetheart, did you hear what the kid said?"

"Yup. His name...both their names, in fact, *are* Jewish names."

"Uh huh. And did you hear the last name of the other kid?"

"Yup. Tamari."

"Uh huh. Gloria, I think we've entered the 'Twilight Zone,' passed through some kind of time warp and are experiencing Colonel Tamari's childhood."

"But Tamari's first name is Asher, Larry. This kid is Moshe."

"It's all the same to me, sweets. I think I need a drink."

The boys started laughing. They were on their way! It was all too crazy. Who were these Americans anyway? And how did they know Colonel Tamari? Larry motioned to the boys to get into the van and during the long drive through Kenya, they all filled each other in on some of the details.

"Boy, what a *mess*," muttered Larry after the boys had recounted their adventures—without giving away the secret of Sambatyon.

"What do you mean by that, Larry?" asked Gloria. "I think it's all a miracle, what they went through, not a mess!"

"That's what I said, sweets. Just practicing my Hebrew some. 'mess' is Hebrew for miracle."

"*Ness*," Moshe corrected him. Everyone laughed but Larry.

"So you ain't gonna tell us how you survived in the jungle

after those guides ran off?" pressed Larry.

"Sorry," replied Simcha. "It's a secret."

"Sure, sure, a secret. I know all about that. Whatcha gonna do, write a book? Maybe sell your story to a magazine or a movie company?"

"Nah. It wasn't anything," said Moshe. "Just survival. We ate some berries, drank a lot of water, and just did our best to save ourselves. Obviously, G-d took care of the rest. G-d sort of met us half way."

"No doubt about that," Gloria interjected. "Just when we came speeding around the bend, so did you guys. Amazing, really amazing. Isn't it, Larry?"

"Yup. A real mess...uh...I mean *ness*."

"Oh my!" Moshe suddenly exclaimed.

"What is it?" asked Gloria, somewhat alarmed.

"Uh... nothing, nothing. I mean...uh...I'm car sick!"

"Me, too!" cried Simcha, realizing almost immediately that they had all but forgotten about the ambush the colonel was headed for together with hundreds of Ethiopian Jewish men, women, and children. The van pulled to the side once more and the boys jumped out and headed toward some nearby bushes. Once out of sight, they huddled in an anxious discussion over what to do.

"How will we get word to my father?" asked Moshe anxiously. "I pray it's not too late."

"Not only that, but how will we warn your father when we're not permitted to reveal the source of our information? He'll never believe us without knowing where we found out about it!"

"But lives are in danger! Anything is permitted!"

"You're right! This is no time to philosophize. We must act now. G-d has helped us this far. I'm sure we'll be met half way again. We have to try our best."

"Wait!" cried Moshe, "I got it! I got it!"

"You've got what?"

"An idea! The ants!"

"The ants? I don't understand, Moshe. What about the ants?"

"I've no time to explain right now. Let's get back to the van. Just leave everything to me."

"It's about time. I could use a vacation!" said Simcha with a sigh.

Once inside the van, Moshe engaged Larry and Gloria in casual conversation about the route his father was taking to get to the Kenya-Ethiopia border. Apparently, Larry and the other Californians were to converge with Tamari not far from the border to drive the Ethiopian Jewish refugees from there to a landing field, where Israeli planes would be waiting.

As they spoke, Gloria pulled out a map of the area to show the boys exactly where the colonel was travelling. Suddenly, Moshe gasped, feigning shock and disbelief. Simcha joined him, although he had no idea what Moshe's scheme was.

"What's the matter now?" asked Gloria, "Car sick again? Larry, take it easy on those curves!"

"No, we're not car sick," explained Moshe, "just worried. We know that area on the map. We were lost just about there yesterday, right, Simcha? Look, there's the beginning of the mountain range we passed, right? And there's that little lake we took a dip in, remember? And all that brush right there! That's the place! That's the place! They must be told to turn back! Immediately! Radio them or something! Quick!"

"Why?" shouted Larry, growing nervous and pulling the van off the road once again.

"Ants! Millions of ants!" screamed Moshe. "Millions of red killer ants are heading directly into his path! He must turn away immediately. He must turn back! We saw them!"

Larry got Tamari on the radio.

"Kode-Kode to *Gafrur*[1]," came Tamari's voice. "What is it?"

"Are you in 'D' zone yet?" asked Larry.

[1]*gafrur*—match [Hebrew]. A safety match with a red striking head.

"Approaching 'D' zone in about fifteen, twenty minutes. Why?"

"Uh... turn back now. Ants headed your way, millions of red killer ants. Find alternative route, over."

"What?! Who told you this? How do you know this?"

"Your boy Moshe. He and his friend are with us. Long story. They were lost in 'C' zone. Claim the ants are headed your way by this time. Over."

"What?! The boys? What kind of tricks are they up to?"

Tamari switched off. Simcha and Moshe looked at one another, Simcha wondering how well a false report about invading ants was going to work, Moshe praying it would work. In ten minutes both received their answer. Tamari radioed the van.

"This is Kode-Kode to all units, Kode-Kode to all units. We are going to have a party in 'D' zone. We know all about the ants now. Everything under control. All units report to 'D' zone for celebration. Bring lots of mustard and champagne. Not you, *Gafrur*. You all stay put. We may need you to bring more mayonnaise. Over!"

"Omigosh!" exclaimed Larry. "All that stuff was code language. Party means war. Champagne means explosives, or shootings. They're preparing for some kind of attack! Maybe bandits!"

Moshe and Simcha looked at one another, cautious relief in their eyes. The plan had worked, and the colonel was preparing to thwart the terrorists' ambush with a surprise attack of his own. Simcha was puzzled, though. How had Moshe's warning about killer ants been translated into a warning about a fatal ambush?

The van picked up speed as it headed toward the preplanned meeting point at the border. Overhead, several military helicopters flew speedily across the nearby border toward the jungle.

CHAPTER 11

Ambush

Colonel Tamari lay face down in the grass. News of the pending guerrilla ambush had caught him by surprise, and now he had to make some hasty decisions. He was relieved that at least the refugees were safe, tucked away in the brush a quarter of a mile away. When he had received the news, Tamari had pulled the trucks off the road and covered them with leaves and branches. He had also left several of his men behind just in case the worst happened and the terrorists discovered the refugees.

Their bodies covered by jungle growth, Tamari and his men were lying very close to where the terrorists were supposed to be waiting in ambush. The colonel awaited word of the RPV he had ordered for the battle. An RPV was a very small airplane, about six feet long and one foot high, flown by remote control. What made the RPV (Remotely Piloted Vehicle) so important to Israeli soldiers was its ability to carry a small video camera which could transmit instant pictures of what was going on below. Such "toy" planes had already helped save hundreds of lives in recent confrontations between Israel and Syria. Instead of risking sending a soldier to observe and report enemy movements, the small pilotless plane had done the job.

Luckily, Israel had several RPVs in Nairobi, which they were using to train their allies in modern warfare. Several miles away from Tamari and his men, Lieutenant Eliyahu Ben Nun was helping three other Israeli agents remove the heavy canvas that covered the RPV sitting on the back of his truck. The pilotless plane was attached to a rocket launcher, which Eliyahu wasted no time elevating into position, aiming the RPV in the direction of Tamari and the guerrillas. He then climbed back into the cabin of the truck—where the remote controls were—and began to launch. The others stepped back several yards as the RPV shot off the truck like a missile, soaring high into the air. The lieutenant now turned on the small television screen in the cabin and got a bird's eye view of the jungle as relayed by the RPV's camera. He slowly turned a knob on the right side of the screen to zoom in the RPV's lens for a closer look at the ground.

Suddenly, a red light began flickering on and off on the screen. The RPV had detected the radio frequency of the enemy's communications equipment. Eliyahu directed the RPV to the area from which the radio had been detected. At the same time, he pushed several other buttons on the side of the screen, immediately jamming the frequency over which the guerrillas were transmitting.

Once the enemy's radio was jammed, Eliyahu safely contacted Tamari by walkie-talkie. "Kode-Kode," Eliyahu called.

"'Kode-Kode' to you, too," Tamari shot back.

"You can speak freely now, Colonel. I've got their communications jammed, and I'm beginnging to zero in on their location."

"It's about time, Eliyahu. I've been lying here for a half hour, and I've become a major conference center for ants and beetles."

"You okay otherwise?"

"Besides ants in my pants, I'm okay. I have eight men with

me, and we are waiting to move in. We are located approximately thirty yards from the road, alongside the creek.

"Can I get you anything, Colonel?"

"Yes, a pastrami sandwich with lots of mustard," quipped Tamari sarcastically.

It didn't take long for the RPV's camera to pick up the positions of both Tamari's men and the guerrillas. To the guerrillas, the small aircraft overhead probably seemed like an ordinary plane flying high in the sky. To Eliyahu it meant immediate information on exactly where each and every guerrilla lay, stood, or sat, and the kinds of weapons they were carrying.

"Okay, Tamari," Eliyahu whispered across the radio. "Approximately a hundred yards northeast at 30-degrees from your position there is a .50 caliber machinegun mounted behind a boulder and manned by two guerrillas. About ten feet to the left of them are six men with automatic rifles. Behind them are two men with rocket launchers and a third, who appears to be a leader of some sort, armed with a handgun and a Russian rifle. They seem to be facing the direction of the road, expecting you to pass. I am turning the RPV around for a more definite picture, just to make sure. Aha! Three more men are now emerging from a cave. Beware of possible guerrillas in a cave twenty-or-so feet off the road. One of them is carrying the jammed radio on his back. He sure must be wondering why it isn't working! He's coming out of the cave and walking toward the leader. They're all yours, Tamari."

"Thanks, Eliyahu."

Tamari motioned to his men to move forward, and he led them stealthily through the thick jungle brush. He sent some across the nearby road, and others he ordered to approach the guerrillas from behind. His plan, thanks to the RPV, was simply to ambush the ambush. The men, their faces and arms painted with various shades of green and brown, moved quickly through the brush, their Uzi submachineguns poised. Each man carried a walkie-talkie and kept in touch with Tamari.

"Spread apart now," the colonel ordered. The men moved farther from one another as they drew closer to where the guerrillas were waiting. "Don't shoot unless you have to. I want prisoners. I want to know who's behind all this. I want their leader. And don't take any chances either."

The Israeli agents were now only yards away from the guerrillas. They stopped suddenly, quietly assumed a crawling position, and waited for Tamari to give them the green light. The guerrillas were completely surrounded.

"Now!" Tamari shouted. His troops jumped to their feet and drew their Uzis.

Bewildered and screaming, the guerrillas fired in all directions, unable to determine where the Israeli agents were firing from. Tamari shouted in Arabic to the guerrillas to surrender. But they continued throwing grenades and firing their guns blindly. Some tried to flee but were met by Tamari's agents who were in position along the road. Amid the blind shooting, Tamari and two other agents moved quickly toward the cave Eliyahu had mentioned. They threw several tear-gas grenades inside. Three guerrillas ran from the cave coughing and wheezing. Tamari and his agents quickly captured and handcuffed them.

In minutes the battle was over. Eliyahu brought up the truck to load the prisoners.

CHAPTER 12

Of Puzzles and Secrets

Colonel Tamari embraced Moshe and Simcha as he climbed into the rear of Larry and Gloria's van. Several of the newly liberated refugees climbed in as well, while others filled the vans belonging to Larry's friends and several trucks driven by Tamari's aides. Eliyahu's military truck whizzed by the convoy. Inside it, armed Kenyan soldiers guarded a number of dazed and defeated Palestinian terrorists, who sat on the floor of the truck, their hands tied behind their backs. Among them sat Samoa, his military rank and insignia ripped from his uniform.

As the convoy of refugees and rescuers headed for the airfield, Tamari interrogated the boys about their experiences, but could only get them to explain how they got lost in the jungle, not how they got back out. The story behind their survival was cloaked in hems and haws and quick, brief responses that only made the colonel more and more curious.

"Funny thing about those ants you claimed were headed our way," Tamari said as the van veered off the main highway onto a dirt road. "They never showed up. I wonder why."

The boys remained silent.

"Another funny thing about those uh… ants, is that as soon as I told my head guide, Samoa, that the ants were coming and that he had to find us a different route, he became really nervous. He started sweating and trembling. He insisted we continue on; that we shouldn't worry about the ants. He seemed rather in a hurry to move to the 'D' zone, and that made me suspicious. I didn't make colonel for nothing, you know," Tamari said, throwing a sharp glance at the boys. "Anyway, the more I insisted we turn back, the more anxious he became."

Simcha smiled. He now understood the process of Moshe's trick. How clever!

"So I asked him why he was so nervous," Tamari went on. "When he didn't answer, I ordered his shoulder pack searched. Then he reached for his pistol—which told me all I needed to know. He was leading me into a trap. We pulled back right there, took cover, and radioed for local military aid."

The boys remained silent, listening attentively and showing great interest in Tamari's story.

"But the ants," the colonel continued, eyeing the boys suspiciously, "never showed up."

Tamari waited for the boys to respond, but they remained silent.

"Did you really see millions of red killer ants?"

"Uh huh," they said.

"You know," he went on, "you two have been a great help to me in solving several mysteries before. I only hope that one day you'll help me solve the biggest puzzle of all."

"What's that, Abba?" Moshe asked.

"The two of you. Two little puzzle pieces I can't seem to figure out."

The boys grinned.

The airfield was now in sight. Three camouflaged planes

waited, engines roaring and propellers spinning. To the side of the field sat a helicopter, its blades whirring.

"We'll be returning to Nairobi by chopper," Tamari shouted above the din. "But...uh...I must ask you two—please, please— do not tell Esther that you got lost during the safari, okay? You think you can keep a secret, boys?"

Simcha and Moshe winked at one another.

"Yes," they said in unison. "We can keep a secret."